LAUGH YOUR SOCKS OFF WITH

# Jeremy STRONG

# Pandemonium at School

Illustrated by

## Judy Brown

PUFFIN

*For Jane: A great friend and a*
*brilliant teacher, without whom this*
*story could never have existed.*

PUFFIN BOOKS

Published by the Penguin Group
Penguin Books Ltd, 80 Strand, London WC2R ORL, England
Penguin Group (USA) Inc., 375 Hudson Street, New York, New York 10014, USA
Penguin Group (Canada), 90 Eglinton Avenue East, Suite 700, Toronto, Ontario, Canada M4P 2Y3
(a division of Pearson Penguin Canada Inc.)
Penguin Ireland, 25 St Stephen's Green, Dublin 2, Ireland (a division of Penguin Books Ltd)
Penguin Group (Australia), 250 Camberwell Road, Camberwell, Victoria 3124, Australia
(a division of Pearson Australia Group Pty Ltd)
Penguin Books India Pvt Ltd, 11 Community Centre, Panchsheel Park, New Delhi – 110 017, India
Penguin Group (NZ), 67 Apollo Drive, Rosedale, Auckland 0632, New Zealand
(a division of Pearson New Zealand Ltd)
Penguin Books (South Africa) (Pty) Ltd, 24 Sturdee Avenue, Rosebank, Johannesburg 2196, South Africa

Penguin Books Ltd, Registered Offices: 80 Strand, London WC2R ORL, England

puffinbooks.com

First published by A & C Black (Publishers) Ltd 1990
First published in Puffin Books 1999
Published in this edition 2011
001 – 10 9 8 7 6 5 4 3 2 1

Text copyright © Jeremy Strong, 1990
Illustrations copyright © Judy Brown, 1990
All rights reserved

The moral right of the author and illustrator has been asserted

Set in Monotype Baskerville
Made and printed in Great Britain by Clays Ltd, St Ives plc

Except in the United States of America, this book is sold subject to the condition
that it shall not, by way of trade or otherwise, be lent, re-sold, hired out, or otherwise
circulated without the publisher's prior consent in any form of binding or cover other than
that in which it is published and without a similar condition including this condition
being imposed on the subsequent purchaser

British Library Cataloguing in Publication Data
A CIP catalogue record for this book is available from the British Library

ISBN: 978–0–141–33617–6

www.greenpenguin.co.uk

MIX
Paper from
responsible sources
FSC
www.fsc.org   FSC™ C018179

Penguin Books is committed to a sustainable
future for our business, our readers and our
planet. This book is made from paper certified
by the Forest Stewardship Council.

# Contents

| RENFREWSHIRE COUNCIL | |
| --- | --- |
| 180317521 | |
| Bertrams | 26/08/2011 |
| | £6.99 |
| RAL | |

# 1 The New Teacher

There was a long, long silence during which time Mr Shrapnell stared dully at the telephone still dangling in his left hand. Slowly he raised his eyes until they met those of Mrs Bunt, the school secretary. She put a thin hand to her mouth, already anxious.

'Oh, Mr Shrapnell, what is the matter? Who was that on the phone?'

For the first time the Headmaster seemed to become aware of the machine that had brought the bad news. He carefully replaced it on the receiver and raised his eyes to Mrs Bunt again, spearing her with a steel-grey glare. 'That was Mr David, Mrs Bunt. He went sleepwalking last night, fell downstairs and broke his arm and two ribs.'

'Oh the poor man. The poor, poor man!' cried Mrs Bunt, not even noticing that the Headteacher had clamped his jaws together and seemed to be grinding his teeth with grim fury. Mrs Bunt had now clasped both hands in an attitude of deep prayer. 'The poor man. What he must be suffering, and him with his bad back too.'

Mr Shrapnell could take no more. He sprang to his feet and strode round his desk. 'I don't care how many broken legs or bad backs he's got, Mrs Bunt! I don't care if he's been sawn in half, stuffed with green peppers and eaten by gourmet cannibals from the depths of Borneo. I don't care, I don't care – as long as he arrives every day by ten minutes to nine and teaches his class of thirty-two nine year olds. That is his job, Mrs Bunt, do you understand?'

The secretary really was trembling now.
It was at times like these that she
wondered why she continued to work for
Mr Shrapnell. His rages were so
unpredictable. It was like walking blindfold
across a minefield. It was also at times like
these she remembered children with cut
knees, grazed elbows and scratches in the
most unexpected places. Then there were
the lumps and bumps she had smoothed

and the tears she had wiped dry, and she knew why she carried on working at Dullandon Primary School.

Mr Shrapnell leaned towards her, his right eye beginning to twitch in one corner. He glared over her shoulder to the wall behind and stabbed at it with a thick finger.

'Do you see that, Mrs Bunt? It's the school timetable. That is what the school works to. Look, look! Monday, May the third. There it is – see? There!'

The secretary nodded quickly as Mr Shrapnell almost pushed her face into the timetable. 'And see here, this is Mr David's class on Monday, May the third. Maths, English, History and then –' the Headteacher lowered his voice to a grave whisper – 'Science, Mrs Bunt, Science.' For a moment he was lost in thought, then he turned back to the secretary. 'Now, tell me, Mrs Bunt, who is going to teach Mr David's class today? Or tomorrow? Or the day after that? He will be away from school for at least a week. It's a disaster!' The Head gave a shudder at the thought of such selfishness on the part of the injured Mr David.

The school secretary calmed herself. 'I'll get on the phone at once Mr Shrapnell. I'm sure we can find a replacement for poor Mr David.'

'And stop calling him poor!' yelled the Head, as she hurried back to her office. 'He's going to destroy the running of the school. I've spent months perfecting that timetable!' She heard his door slam shut and sat down on her chair with relief.

'One day,' she promised herself, 'I am going to tell Mr Shrapnell just what I think of him. Now, let's try Mrs Perkins. She's filled in for us before.' But there was no reply from Mrs Perkins. 'Well how about Miss Juniper?'

This time there was an answer, but when Miss Juniper heard that Dullandon Primary School was a teacher short she almost spat down the phone. 'You can tell Mr Shrapnell to go and boil his head,' she told Mrs Bunt. 'I'll not work for that old ratbag again!'

'I know just how you feel,' murmured Mrs Bunt as she dialled Mr Dunwoody's number. But Mr Dunwoody had retired from teaching altogether. Mrs Bunt tried four more supply teachers but they all had an excuse or they were out. Mrs Bunt began to get the impression that nobody wanted to come near the school and she had almost run out of names on her list.

The door was suddenly flung open and
Mr Shrapnell's angry head appeared.
'Have you got someone yet, Mrs Bunt?
School starts in ten minutes.'

'I'm afraid Mrs Perkins can't come, Miss
Juniper is, er, otherwise engaged, Mr
Dunwoody has —'

'Don't give me feeble excuses, woman.
This is an emergency. Find me a teacher
for Mr David's class.' The door slammed
shut whipping a pile of papers from Mrs
Bunt's desk and scattering them across the
carpet.

The secretary got down on her hands
and knees and searched for the list of
supply teachers. At last it was found,
beneath the caretaker's order for six tons
of lavatory cleaner. Mrs Bunt groaned. 'I
do wish the caretaker would spell things
properly.' She crossed out the 'o' in tons

and changed it to six tins. 'I should think six tons would last us about a hundred years. Now, who's left on this list – Mrs Green and Miss Pandemonium.'

The secretary picked up the phone again. There was no answer from Mrs Green and that left Miss Pandemonium. The phone had hardly rung once before it was answered at the other end by a very excited voice.

'Don't you worry,' gabbled Miss Pandemonium. 'I shall be over in a jiffy. No – even quicker than that – in a jiff! I'll grab my bag and dash upstairs and put on some make-up – no I won't – I'll do that in the van on the way over. My goodness, school starts in five minutes. I shall have to get a move on.'

'Miss Pandemonium,' began Mrs Bunt. 'Do you know the –'

'Dunderbank School, isn't it?' shouted Miss Pandemonium down the telephone. Her voice came over in a very odd way because she was hopping about on one foot while she was talking, trying to pull on one half of a pair of tights.

'Are you all right?' Mrs Bunt inquired anxiously, as a huge crash rolled down the telephone line and fell into her right ear.

'Fine! Fine!' Miss Pandemonium's voice sounded a bit distant. This was probably because she had fallen one way and the telephone had whizzed off in the opposite direction. 'Don't worry, I'm on my way,' announced Miss Pandemonium, and the phone went dead before Mrs Bunt had time to tell her that the school was called Dullandon, not Dunderbank.

Mrs Bunt gave her head a little shake as if to get some sense back into it. She rose from her seat to go and tell the Headmaster, then paused for a second. A tiny smile found its way on to her thin lips. She had a feeling about Miss Pandemonium, the sort of feeling that made her feel nervous and just a bit giggly. Heaven alone knew why she should feel like that. Perhaps it was the thought of Mr Shrapnell meeting the new teacher.

Anyhow, the Head was delighted to hear the news. He glanced at his watch. 'Four, no, three minutes to go before the whistle for the start of school. Well done, Mrs Bunt. Let's hope she can get here in time. What do we know about her?'

Mrs Bunt glanced at the list of supply teachers. 'She says here that she will teach anything to anyone.'

The Head rubbed his hands together. 'Indeed? Good, good. I hope she gets a

move on. I must go and blow the whistle.'
He grabbed a whistle from the back of his
door and strode across the hall to the
playground.

The children were screaming and
shouting and dashing round like the balls
in a pinball machine. But the children
meant little to Mr Shrapnell. He ran the
school like his own private army. There
was a place for everything, and everything
in its place. There was a time for
everything, and everything . . . his eyes
were on his watch. Ten seconds, nine,
eight – the whistle was in his mouth at the
ready.

A piercing shrill brought the rush and
dash and noise to a halt. Every child stood
stock still, frozen to the spot. 'Frazer! Your
foot moved. Stand still, boy! That girl
there, yes you, stop scratching!'

Mr Shrapnell glanced across to the car park. Still no sign of Miss Pandemonium. From the distance came the faint sound of a siren. Probably a fire engine, he noted mentally. He began to call out the names of classes. Lines of children filed silently into school. The siren came closer. Some children turned to see if it would pass by the school gates. Would it be a fire engine or a police car?

There was a screech of tyres at the corner of the road and an ambulance veered into view. Lights were flashing and the siren wee-wahed furiously. It whizzed past the school while everyone stared. Not even Mr Shrapnell could resist the thrill.

The ambulance suddenly screeched to a halt and reversed, its siren still screaming. A side window flew open and an arm shot out, making a grand signal for a right turn.

Then the ambulance growled, scrunged its gears, leaped forward down the school drive and skidded to a halt in the car park.

A short figure jumped out, pulling six assorted bags after her and spilling half of them on to the tarmac. She gazed around for a moment and ran a hand through a head of hair that looked like a rook's nest. She had lipstick halfway up one cheek and eyeshadow over most of her nose. She gave Mr Shrapnell a cheery grin and staggered across the playground towards him, trailing bags behind.

'Morning!' she cried. 'What a lovely morning too – Violet Pandemonium – how do you do?'

'But, but,' began Mr Shrapnell. 'That ambulance –'

'Smashing isn't it? I bought it at a car

auction last year. Everything still works you know, siren, lights, the lot!'

'I heard,' muttered Mr Shrapnell.

'Shall we go in? No time to waste,' said Miss Pandemonium. 'Lead on, Macduff – that's Shakespeare you know.'

Mr Shrapnell gave a low groan and

trailed behind Miss Pandemonium into the
school, picking up all the bits she dropped
as she went.

# 2 The Great Dart Contest

'This is Class Three,' said Mr Shrapnell.
Thirty-two children sat silent and still,
staring first at their new teacher, then at
Mr Shrapnell, and finally, irresistibly back
at the new teacher. 'Class Three, this is
Miss Pandemonium.'

Violet Pandemonium gave the class a
big smile and dropped another two of her
bags. 'Good morning, everyone!' she sang
and immediately disappeared beneath the
tables to pick up her belongings.

'Good Mor-ning Miss-Pan-dee-moh-
nee-umm,' chanted Class Three, even
though she had vanished from their sight.

'Mr David is ill,' grunted Mr Shrapnell.
'However, I am sure you are in good hands

with Miss Pandemonium here. Oh, by the way, Miss Pandemonium, the timetable is pinned to the wall there. I think Maths comes first.'

'What's that?' came a faint voice from somewhere beneath the tables. 'Oooh, I've found a rubber that looks like an elephant. Anyone lost an elephant?' A hand appeared above the desk-tops waving a little pink rubber. 'Who's lost an elephant?'

Mr Shrapnell stared at the creature and the arm quite speechless. He had never

heard anything like it. As for Class Three, they were dumbstruck too. They waited breathlessly, expecting Mr Shrapnell to explode at any moment. But he didn't. He just stared at the thin hand waving the rubber elephant. Then Miss Pandemonium's face appeared as she clambered back to her feet. 'Come on, it must belong to someone,' she said brightly. 'Poor little elephant without a home.'

There was a faint snigger from the back of the class. Mr Shrapnell whirled round and glared into the depths of the classroom. He drew in his breath sharply. 'I shall leave you to it, Miss Pandemonium, and don't forget – Maths!'

Mr Shrapnell strode to the door and disappeared. There was a sigh of relief and the children slumped back in their chairs. Violet Pandemonium looked at them carefully. They gazed back at her with a dull expression in their eyes. Three of them were already looking in their desks.

'What are you doing?' asked Miss Pandemonium.

'Getting out our Maths books, miss.'

'Who said anything about Maths?' she asked gently. The three heads reappeared and eyed her carefully.

'We always do Maths on Monday,' said Rebecca.

'I see, well, we mustn't change the timetable, must we? Is this it over here?' Miss Pandemonium screwed up her eyes to read the vast sheet of paper which was covered with blue writing. There were lots of bits underlined with red. 'That does look interesting,' she said at last. 'Now then, Maths. Let's see, what's your name?'

'Peter, miss.'

'All right, Peter – what's two add two?'

Peter groaned with boredom. 'Four, miss.'

'Well done. And who are you?'

'Amy, miss.'

'Amy, what is six hundred and ninety-two, add five thousand two hundred and sixty, divided by eight?'

It was Amy's turn to groan. That was hopelessly hard to do in her head. 'Don't know, miss,' she whispered, and waited for a scream of anger.

'Neither do I,' smiled Miss Pandemonium. 'But it must be an awful lot. Well then, that's got our Maths done for the day. What do we do next?'

'It says English on the timetable, miss,' Amber called out.

'In that case please tell the class how to spell "cat".' Amber duly spelled the word.

'That's lovely,' said Miss Pandemonium. 'Now we've done our English. History next, I believe. Anthony, when's your birthday?'

'October the twenty-eighth, miss.'

Violet Pandemonium glanced at her watch. 'Half-past nine and we've done the whole timetable!'

'We haven't done Science yet,' groaned Luke.

'We're always doing Science,' moaned Wayne.

The classroom door burst open and Mr Shrapnell poked his big head round the frame. 'Everything all right, Miss Pandemonium?' he snapped. 'Maths?'

'Doing it, Mr Shrapnell,' said Miss Pandemonium cheerfully. For a moment the two adults looked at each other. It seemed as if Mr Shrapnell did not believe her and she was waiting for him to say more. Meantime she just gazed at him steadily with her bright, grey eyes. Mr Shrapnell found the stare rather unnerving. He gave a curt nod, quietly pulled the door shut and went away.

Miss Pandemonium turned back to the class. 'Tell me what science you have done so far this term, Mark.'

'We've been doing a topic on birds, miss.'

'Have you? That sounds like fun.'

'We've done finches and ducks and gulls so far,' Mark went on, rather listlessly.

Miss Pandemonium now had her head buried deep inside one of her bags. 'If you carry on like that,' a muffled voice said from the bottom of the bag, 'you should have covered the whole bird kingdom in about two years' time. Ah, that's what I was after. Paul, give a sheet of this paper to everyone. Now, who can tell me what origami is?'

'Is she a pop star, miss?' asked Kerry.

'That's brilliant! What a wonderful name! Actually origami is a Japanese word and it means the art of folding paper. Paul's just given you a sheet of origami paper and I want you to fold it into a triangle, like this.'

Everyone busily folded their sheet. The door whizzed open. 'Maths?' inquired Mr Shrapnell, glaring suspiciously.

'Hold up your shapes, Class Three,' cried Miss Pandemonium. 'What are they?'

'Triangles!' shouted the class.

Mr Shrapnell frowned, growled, shut the door and went away. The children looked at each other and grinned. This was great.

'Now fold here. Bend that tip like so. Good, now squash the square section, turn it over and push in this angle here and there – you have a bird. Easy, wasn't it?'

There was a whisper of excitement as Class Three realized what they had just done, but Miss Pandemonium hadn't finished. 'Take the legs that are hanging down and pull gently – there!'

'Wow!' cried Karen. 'It flaps! It flaps its wings when you pull the legs!' Thirty-two origami birds were flapping about over the desktops. A rising chorus of bird calls began to fill the classroom. Miss Pandemonium joined in enthusiastically, climbing on to her desk and making her bird dive down.

'I'm a kestrel,' she cried. 'Keeaw! Keeeaw! Look out, John, you've just laid an egg!'

John smiled. 'Are you, sort of, well, mad, miss?' Violet stood up straight, thought for a moment and then jumped down.

'Quite possibly,' she told him. He smiled again.

'I thought you were,' he said happily.

'OK, birds down for a second,' Miss Pandemonium called. 'Who can tell me how birds fly?'

'Someone pulls their legs, miss!' shouted Wayne.

'I don't think so,' she laughed. She dug into her bag again and pulled out more origami paper. 'Make a paper dart that will go as far as possible,' said Miss Pandemonium.

Lee shifted uneasily. 'We're not allowed darts.'

'Has anyone told you not to make paper *aeroplanes*?'

'Only darts, miss,' grinned Jackie, hurriedly beginning to fold her paper into a supersonic mach-twelve aeroplane.

A few minutes later, darts were whizzing around the classroom and Miss Pandemonium called a halt. She took the class through to the hall where there was plenty of room, but throwing them across the hall was not good enough for Miss Pandemonium.

'We need more height. Pull those wall bars out. Seabirds launch themselves off clifftops, so the wall bars can be our cliff. That's it, smashing! Come on, everyone.'

Miss Pandemonium clambered up the side of the climbing frame and a host of children swarmed after her, clutching their darts.

'I always wanted to be a seabird when I was small,' said Violet. 'I wanted to be an

albatross. I wish I'd been born an
albatross.'

'Did you, miss?' Theresa looked at her
teacher quizzically. Miss Pandemonium
seemed ever so strange, but there was
something nice and comfortable about her
too. Theresa was prompted to say
something she had never told anyone. 'I've
always wanted to be a rabbit,' she
whispered.

'Oh, how lovely! And here we are. Right
everybody, one at a time – launch your
aeroplanes.'

One by one the children threw their

darts. Some did splendid nosedives straight into the hall floor. Some curved upwards at high speed and then slowly twirled round and round and down. Only two or three actually flew some distance, and as each throw took place it was carefully measured with a long tape.

Miss Pandemonium had made a dart of her own. It whizzed straight back over her shoulder and crashed into the wall behind. 'Oh dear, mine's gone backwards.' Class Three were laughing.

'Miss Pandemonium! What is all this noise?' Mr Shrapnell stood at the other end of the hall, glaring angrily at the floor which was covered with darts of all sizes. 'What on earth is going on here? Children, you know darts are NOT allowed.'

Miss Pandemonium grabbed a nearby rope and slid down to the bristling

Headteacher. 'Mr Shrapnell, we are making a serious investigation into the nature of flight. How can we do work on Birds without understanding the principle of flight? Look at my one. It's just flown backwards.' She thrust the dart into Mr Shrapnell's hands. 'Now, can you tell me why it went backwards? Watch.' She snatched it back, threw it, and once again it vanished over her shoulder. 'See? I told you so.'

Mr Shrapnell picked up the dart. He began to smooth one of the wings. 'I think it's because the . . .' He stopped suddenly and frowned angrily. 'Miss Pandemonium, this is not on the timetable and I don't think you should encourage children to –'

'This is Science, isn't it?' interrupted Violet, watching the Head with those bright, grey eyes again. 'I think Julie's dart has gone the furthest, so she's won. We'll go back to class and see if we can discover why her dart worked best. Would you like to come and help, Mr Shrapnell?'

The Head stepped back in horror and muttered something darkly about far too much work. Miss Pandemonium smiled and took the children back to class. As they went, Rebecca whispered to the others, 'I hope Miss P stays for ever and ever. She's brilliant!'

But Glenn was more thoughtful. 'She won't last long. You saw the way Shrapnoodle looked at her. He's going to get rid of her as soon as possible and then it will be back to the old boring ways. You wait and see.'

# 3 To Fly Like A Bird – Almost

'Miss Pandemonium,' began Mr Shrapnell, pacing back and forth behind his desk. 'You must understand the importance of rules. The children must do what you tell them to do.'

Violet smiled. 'That's why I'm so pleased, Mr Shrapnell. They're lovely children and they did exactly as I asked.'

Mr Shrapnell stopped pacing, stared at the ceiling as if it had just blown a raspberry at him, then turned to the new teacher. 'I beg your pardon, Miss Pandemonium?'

'Please, call me Violet. I was named after the flower you know. Mother always thought of me as a shrinking violet. I can't imagine why. I've always thought of myself as more like a dandelion, although of course that wouldn't sound quite right would it – Dandelion Pandemonium?'

'Miss Dandymonium!' yelled the Head. 'Please pay attention. Are you telling me you actually *asked* the children to make paper darts, climb the wall bars and fly them across the hall?'

'Yes, of course!'

'But there is nothing on the timetable about using the hall at that time. You were supposed to be doing English.' Miss Pandemonium gave the Head a curious glance. What a strange person he must be to let life be ruled by a timetable. 'You were supposed to be doing English. Instead, you asked the children to deliberately break the school rules and fly paper darts round the hall!'

'There wasn't enough room in class,' said Miss Pandemonium.

'You asked them to make paper darts! You might just as well have got them making helicopters or something equally stupid!'

Miss Pandemonium leaped to her feet. 'Helicopters! Mr Shrapnell, you are so clever. Here am I, sitting right in front of you and thinking what a silly old man you are, going on about paper darts, as if it mattered, and that silly old timetable too! And all the time you were thinking why waste time on darts when you could be making helicopters!'

'But Miss –' started Mr Shrapnell in horror. However, Violet Pandemonium was now in full flow, and not to be stopped.

'Of course it will be difficult. Making

the rotors won't be easy, and the flap angle will be vital. Oh Mr Shrapnell, you've opened my eyes. Why should we bother with silly old darts when we could really fly? We could really *fly*!' she repeated, and almost ran from the Headmaster's office.

Mr Shrapnell slumped back. He could not understand how she got away with it. Every time he pointed out what was wrong, it got twisted round until he didn't know what she would do or say next. What on earth was she up to now? He groaned loudly and buried his face in his hands.

Out in the secretary's office, Mrs Bunt heard the groan. She had caught all the conversation before as well. Now she was sitting in front of her typewriter and smiling quietly to herself. All her instincts

about Miss Pandemonium were proving
true, and Mrs Bunt was enjoying every
minute of it.

When the children returned to class after
lunch they found Miss Pandemonium up
to her knees in a pile of junk and looking
very excited. There were bits of balsa
wood and thin steel rods. There were

wheels, cogs, wires, batteries and bulbs. There were thin sticks, thick sticks and bits of string and tape.

Mr David's class stared at the jumble and whispered to each other. Miss Pandemonium suddenly stopped talking to herself and noticed the class for the first time. 'Ah! There you are! Afternoon, everyone.'

'Good Arf-ter-noon-Miss-Pan-dee –'

'Just call me Superwoman,' laughed Miss Pandemonium.

'Superwoman?' giggled Caroline.

'Yes, Superwoman, because this afternoon we are going to fly!'

'FLY!!' chorused Class Three.

'Exactly. Now, how many of you have a bicycle at school?'

Several hands went up. Violet counted and nodded at the same time. 'That's fine.

OK, if you've got a bicycle bring it over to the wall outside the classroom.'

Cheryl looked at her feet and began to mutter that bikes had to stay in the bike shed at all times. Miss Pandemonium ran a hand through her bird's nest of hair and fixed Cheryl with a twinkling pair of eyes. 'My dear, don't worry. Only a little while ago the Headmaster himself was telling me that children must do exactly as they are told. So, please fetch your bikes over to the wall there. Off you go.'

The children did not need to be told again and shortly there were nine bicycles propped up against the wall. They looked at them gravely. Kerry spoke up first.

'Please, miss, if we're going to fly, why do we need bikes?'

'Very good question, Kerry,' said Miss Pandemonium. 'Now I shall ask you one.

How does Man get himself into the air?'

'He jumps!' shouted Luke.

'Not quite the answer I expected but yes, he could jump. But how does he manage to stay up there if he wants to?'

'He goes in an aeroplane,' said John.

'Or a rocket, or a balloon,' Kelly added.

'Or a helicopter,' murmured Paul.

'Exactly,' nodded Miss Pandemonium.

'He doesn't usually go on a bicycle,' Rebecca pointed out.

'That is where you are quite wrong. What we are going to do is turn those bicycles into helicopters. You will climb on board, pedal quickly and the helicopter rotor blades will turn round and up you will go.' Miss Pandemonium spoke so confidently she could have persuaded a bumblebee that it could fly to Mars.

There was a moment's silence. The

whole class looked through the window at the ordinary everyday bicycles leaning against the wall. All at once they gave a yell of delight and dived into the pile of bits and pieces at Miss Pandemonium's feet, while she called out helpful bits of advice.

A great noise of hammering and sawing began. Some children got huge sheets of paper and began to draw out strange plans for their flying machine. Miss Pandemonium got so involved in answering questions that she could not sit back and watch. She was soon down on her hands and knees, helping one of the groups sort out a tricky problem with the rear cog and chain on the bicycle wheel.

Slowly the flying machines began to take shape and the children moved outside to get the rotors fixed. There were some

difficult problems to overcome and there
was glue and tape everywhere. You
couldn't put a foot down anywhere
without treading on something which stuck
to it for the next ten minutes.

Five of the children seemed to have
somehow got themselves completely tied
up with string. It was most strange because
all the knots were right behind their backs
where they could not possibly have
reached for themselves.

'It was Wayne!' cried Amy. 'He did it on purpose.'

'They were no help. They kept getting in the way. I had to tie them up to keep them out of trouble.'

'I think you can release them now,' suggested Miss Pandemonium. 'There, I think we've finished. It's time to put them to the test.'

The bikes made an odd collection. Everyone had found a different way of fixing the rotors above the pilot's head. Some had used thin sticks. Others had used wire rods and string. Now the pilots carefully wheeled their helibikes into the playground, the long rotor blades drooping and bouncing gently as they took up position. The rest of the class watched in silence, wondering if their machines would really fly. Even

Miss Pandemonium was holding her breath.

The pilots climbed on to the saddles. One by one, very slowly and carefully they began to pedal round the playground. The rotor blades circled slowly above their heads, making a low whooshing noise as they sliced the air. The pilots strained over the handlebars to get up speed.

It was hard work pushing those pedals round. They not only drove the rear wheel of the bike but the rotors as well.

'Come on!' cried Miss Pandemonium. 'Pedal faster!' Her words started the rest of the class yelling.

'Faster! Get moving! Come on, Concorde, faster, faster!'

The poor pilots were puffing and panting. Now they stood hard on the

pedals. Sshwish, sshwish went the rotors.
Round and round went the helibikes.

'Take care!' cried Miss Pandemonium.
'Don't let your rotor blades touch one
another.'

There were nine very red faces out on
the playground. One helibike was almost
up in the air. Its front wheel kept lifting
from the ground as if it wanted to take off

but couldn't quite make it. Unfortunately, having one wheel half off the ground made it difficult to steer and very soon one helibike had got too close to another.

The blades met. There was a sharp crack and a large bit of rotor went slicing across the playground and smashed against the school wall. The bikes fell sideways and knocked down another two machines. The other helibikes swerved away violently to avoid the pile-up and smashed head-on into each other. Within seconds the playground had become a major disaster area.

'Oh dear,' murmured Miss Pandemonium, looking anxiously at the pile of wreckage. 'Is everyone all right?'

'Wow!' breathed one of the pilots. 'That was great!'

A loud voice bellowed across the

playground and made everyone (except Miss Pandemonium, of course) freeze on the spot. 'Miss Pandemonium! What on earth is going on out here?'

'We've been making helicopters, Mr Shrapnell.'

'Helicopters? Helicopters! What an utterly ridiculous idea!'

Violet Pandemonium turned and fixed Mr Shrapnell with a pair of innocent grey eyes. 'Oh but, Mr Shrapnell, surely you haven't forgotten? It was *your* idea!'

The Headteacher's jaw dropped open. Once again he was speechless.

# 4  The Very Friendly Cake

Mrs Bunt no longer felt a twinge of fear when she walked through to the Headmaster's office the next morning. She did not quite know why this was, but she did notice and it sent a little warm glow around her insides. She knew Mr Shrapnell was angry. She realized he might well do one of his volcanic eruptions at any moment, but somehow it no longer worried her. She calmly waited for him to speak, and speak he did.

'It is quite dreadful, Mrs Bunt. Surely you can find someone to replace Miss Pandemonium. She is causing chaos.'

'I shall try, Mr Shrapnell. By the way, how is poor Mr David?'

'I've told you before not to call him poor. As far as I understand he is lying in bed with his feet up. He ought to be ashamed of himself. Now, Mrs Bunt, would you please get on the telephone and find someone quiet and sensible instead of that madwoman in Class Three, before she has the whole school falling down round our ears. We must get rid of her as soon as possible.'

Mrs Bunt had to bite her lips to stop a smile spreading across her face. 'I shall see what I can do.'

The sound of a wailing siren came nearer and nearer. A few moments later the ambulance careered down the drive and screeched into the car park. The driver's door opened and a pile of plastic tubs, bowls, spoons and knives clattered on to the tarmac, closely followed by Miss

Pandemonium herself. Her hair looked more like an entire heronry now. She saw Mr Shrapnell watching iron-faced at his window, gave him a massive wave and knocked the wing mirror off the ambulance.

Mr Shrapnell hurried through to the secretary's office. 'Have you got a replacement yet, Mrs Bunt?' The secretary put one hand over the telephone mouthpiece as if she was talking to someone and shook her head.

'Sorry, Mr Shrapnell. Not yet.'

The Head grunted and went back to his office. Mrs Bunt put down the phone and giggled. She had no intention of ringing anyone. She felt that Miss Pandemonium was the best thing that had happened to Dullandon Primary School for ages, and

she was not going to bring it to an end if
she could help it.

'What are we going to do today, miss?'
asked Wayne.

'Help empty my ambulance first of all.
Come on everyone.'

There was a long procession out to the
van to help unload. They found it quite
fascinating. Violet let them all have a go at
making the lights flash and the siren wail.
Then Rebecca tried out the stretcher bed.
Wayne discovered all the bandages and was
all for plastering Rebecca there and then,
but Miss Pandemonium said she felt there
had been enough tying up the day before.

Cheryl picked up some tubs and helped
carry them back to class.

'Miss? Is it true that you want to be an
albatross?'

'Of course. What about you?' But the thought of her teacher as a giant seabird was too much for Cheryl and she couldn't answer.

It took a little while to unload the ambulance and carry all the boxes to the classroom. The children were dying to know what was in the tubs. It wasn't long before they found out.

'We're going to do some cooking today,' announced Miss Pandemonium. It was greeted by groans from a group of children.

'Can't we make our helibikes again?'

'I think we've done enough flying for the time being. It will be a nice change to do some cooking.'

'What are we going to cook?' Caroline asked. 'Can we make ice cream?'

Miss Pandemonium thought for a

second. 'I never thought of that. It would be lovely but I haven't got the stuff with me today. How about making some Friendship Cake?'

'Friendship Cake! What's that?'

'It's something people in Germany used to make, and I think they made it in Canada too. We make a special cake using yeast, flour, sugar, milk and water and we share it with everyone else in the school. That's why it's called Friendship Cake. It's nice to share things with your friends.'

Wayne puzzled over this. 'I shared my black eye with a friend once,' he said.

'How on earth did you do that?' asked Miss Pandemonium.

'Well he gave me a black eye first, so I gave him one back.'

When everyone had stopped laughing,

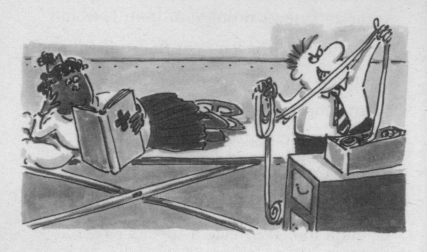

Miss Pandemonium handed round a large
plastic bowl each. Then she put out several
bags of flour, bottles of milk, some big
stirring spoons and finally a large, creamy
brick. The class stared at it.

'What's that?' asked Theresa.

'Yeast. Amazing stuff. It's really alive.'

Luke gave it a poke. 'It's not moving,' he
grunted.

'It's not even breathing,' added Karen.

'I think you should take it to the vet,
miss,' suggested Rebecca.

'It hasn't got eyes or legs. How can it be alive?'

Miss Pandemonium picked it up and started to break off big lumps to hand round the class. 'Yeast is a sort of fungus and –' She was drowned by a chorus of 'Yuck!' from the whole class. They picked up the yeast, sniffed at it and wrinkled their noses in disgust.

'Oh, it's not that bad,' laughed Miss Pandemonium. 'Every loaf of bread has to start off with some yeast in it. It makes the mixture swell up. Get your bowls and put in some flour.'

It wasn't long before most of the desks, and the floor too, were covered in flour. The children had white smudges on their faces, halfway up their arms, and all over their trousers, skirts and jumpers where they had tried to wipe their hands clean.

John somehow managed to sneeze straight into his bowl, sending a cloud of flour billowing across the classroom.

'Urgh!' cried Sarah. 'Don't eat any of that. John's not making Friendship Cake. He's making a Sneeze Cake!'

'Sarah, do you have to be so revolting?' asked Miss Pandemonium. 'Just mix up your flour, milk and water, like this.'

The class began to stir away. Some took it slowly and carefully. It was obvious that they had stirred things before. Others whisked round at several thousand miles per hour and were surprised to discover half the contents flying out over the sides and splurging across the carpet.

'Oops, sorry,' murmured Amber, as her entire bowl took off from her arm, twizzled about in mid-air and fell to the ground, splattering half a dozen children with soggy flour. But everyone was too busy stirring to take much notice.

'Now for the magic ingredient,' announced Miss Pandemonium. 'In goes the yeast.'

'How much should we put in?' asked Kerry.

'Oh, I don't think it matters. When you've done that add plenty of sugar. The yeast needs sugar to feed on. Now work it all together, cover it with a cloth and we'll put it on the heater to help it work. The yeast likes a bit of warmth to get going.'

Each child brought a large bowl of mixture and it was placed by the classroom heater. Miss Pandemonium got some of the children to take bowls to other classes. After all, she explained, it was for sharing with other people. Soon every class in the school had a bowl, or two or three, of Friendship Cake, much to their delight and interest.

Miss Pandemonium even sent some across for Mr Shrapnell and Mrs Bunt. The Headteacher glared at his and pushed it to one side of his desk. Mrs Bunt felt quite honoured.

Back in the classroom there was a strong smell of yeast and flour. 'Hmmm,' sniffed Miss Pandemonium. 'Just like a real bakery, and you are all real bakers,' she added proudly.

The class grinned back at her, covered in flour and paste. They got out their books and began to write about what they had done, while they waited for the yeast to take effect.

'She's really nice,' Karen whispered across to Jackie.

'Shrapnoodle's going to get rid of her,' Glenn warned darkly. 'Anyhow, she's loopy. She wants to be an albatross.'

'So what? I want to be an army tank,' hissed Wayne. 'So just watch it.'

The first sign of success with the mixture came half an hour later when Mark noticed the cloth on his bowl bulging upwards. He took a peek underneath and was surprised to see that the mixture had gone all frothy. Little bubbles kept appearing on the surface and it had risen to the top of the bowl

'That's what the yeast does!' cried Miss Pandemonium excitedly. 'It makes the whole mixture rise.'

'Mine's doing it too!' yelled Julie.

'And mine!'

Right round the class there were yells as they discovered what was happening to their cake. The room was filled with a strong smell of fermenting yeast. Unfortunately the yeast did not stop working once it had reached the top of each bowl. It went bubbling on and on. The truth was that the children had put in far too much yeast, not to mention overdoing the sugar.

The little cloths covering each bowl were rising higher and higher, until you could see the pale, frothing mixture beneath. It looked like a row of bald heads with hankies on top.

Then the bowls started to overflow. The floury paste glooped over the edges and dribbled down to the carpet. There it began to spread, bubbles constantly popping to the surface and releasing the strong gas. The children began to move their desks away from the heater as a slow, smelly tide of flour, milk and water crept towards them.

'Oh dear. I think we may have used too much yeast and sugar,' said Miss Pandemonium quietly.

The same thing was happening in the other classes. The cake was being incredibly friendly and slopping about all over the place. Children were moving out of their classrooms and taking shelter in the hall.

Over in Mr Shrapnell's office, his cake was on the march. It had swept across his desk. Now it was dribbling down all four table legs, carrying several important pieces of paper with it, not to mention five biros of different colours, a stapler and a signed photograph of the Education Minister.

'Mrs Bunt!' he screamed. 'Mrs Bunt! Have you found a replacement yet?'

'Sorry, Mr Shrapnell,' she shouted back. 'I'm afraid Miss Pandemonium will have to carry on.'

She watched the Friendship Cake on her desk carry away the telephone, sat back in her chair and laughed until the tears streamed down her face and she had to hold her sides.

# 5  Not So Friendly After All

'Don't you worry,' Miss Pandemonium told the Headmaster. 'We have made a bit of a mess but —'

'Bit of a mess!' Mr Shrapnell roared. 'Have you looked down the corridors? There are six tons of porridge creeping round the school. It's everywhere!' He tried to pull his hands away from the sticky goo that covered his desk. It clung to his fingers like chewing gum and pulled into long strands.

'It's not porridge,' Miss Pandemonium pointed out. 'It's Friendship Cake. I was going to say that I do realize we have made a bit of a mess and it is our job to clear it up. Don't you worry, Mr Shrapnell.

We shall soon have the whole building spick and span.'

Mr Shrapnell could hardly refuse this polite offer of help, even though a deep instinct warned him that it would only lead to more trouble. But he felt thoroughly tired and did not know how to argue against this awful woman any longer. Besides, for the moment he was far too busy trying to unstick himself.

Miss Pandemonium carefully made her way back to the classroom, her shoes making loud 'skwuck-skwuck' noises as she waded through the Friendship Cake. The children were all huddled together, feeling very nervous and rather scared by the success of their yeast mixture. It didn't take much imagination to work out what Mr Shrapnell must be thinking.

'Well,' began Miss Pandemonium, 'I

think our Friendship Cake has been a little too friendly. That is entirely my fault and I have explained everything to Mr Shrapnell. There is no need for you to worry.'

Luke whispered hoarsely, 'Will you have to go to prison, miss?' He seemed to think that anyone who upset Mr Shrapnell would end up in jail.

'No, of course not. People don't go to prison for little things like this. However, we've made a mess, so it's our job to clear it up.'

'But that will take weeks!' cried Amber. 'We'll be here for ever!'

'Don't you worry. We shall need plenty of hot water and soap powder. We'll need buckets galore and mops and cloths and the vacuum cleaner. Right then, Cleaning Party – Attention!'

The class stood up straight and waited for orders. One group was sent off for mops, another for buckets and water. Some searched for cloths and soap powder. The last three went off to capture the vacuum cleaner and bring it safely back to base camp. It was a dangerous mission. Wherever those children went they had to overcome the terrible creeping cake that was still slowly spreading through the school.

Then the hard work began. Bucket after bucket of hot water was thrown against the oncoming tide. Soap powder was poured on in a white waterfall. The children seized brooms and mops and scrubbed away in their battle against the flour paste. A thick lather of bubbles began to form. The very large ones broke away and drifted slowly down the corridor or

popped against the walls. The foam grew
and grew until it almost reached from
floor to ceiling.

Cheryl and Caroline gave a shout and
vanished right into the bubble mixture.
They reappeared covered in froth that
glistened with all the colours of the
rainbow and did a little dance. Soon
everyone was doing the same. They
walked up and down showing off to their
friends until suddenly they came face to
face with Mr Shrapnell.

For one second the Headmaster thought

aliens from a distant galaxy must have invaded the school.

He almost turned tail and ran for safety. Then he dimly caught sight of Wayne's round face, masked by sparkling bubbles. 'What is the meaning of this?' he hissed.

'Oh, um, sorry, sir,' trembled Wayne, and as he spoke bubbles came from his mouth and floated away. 'We were just trying to clear up the mess.'

'I suppose this was Miss Pandemonium's idea? I'll get rid of her if it's the last thing I do!' His eyes narrowed to thin, dangerous slits. 'Well, was it? Speak up, boy!'

Wayne was silent. He stared at his feet, not that he could see them beneath a thick layer of foam. He just stared at where he thought they were most likely to be found. Mr Shrapnell gritted his teeth, turned on his heel with a loud 'skwuck!' and went to find Miss Pandemonium.

The children started to breathe again. They looked at each other anxiously. 'Poor old Miss P. She's going to catch it,' murmured Theresa. Peter nodded.

'If she goes . . .' he began, but couldn't finish. The others knew what he meant, but even they could not put into words the despair that was chilling their hearts.

'Come on!' cried Anthony. 'At least we can clear this lot up for her!' He grabbed a mop and went back to work. The rest of the class quickly joined in. It was a team effort against the monster cake, and slowly, bit by bit, they began to push back the tide and gain some ground.

Meanwhile, Mr Shrapnell was fighting his way through the building in his search for Miss Pandemonium, determined to bundle her back into the ridiculous ambulance himself, if necessary, and good riddance. He heard a distant whining noise and set off to investigate, only to walk straight into a ceiling-high mass of froth and foam. He plunged on, half blind, until at last he emerged on the other side, squeaky-clean and smothered in bubbles. Through the froth he saw Violet Pandemonium, vacuum cleaner in hand, trying to suck globs of Friendship Cake from the carpet.

'Miss Pandemonium!' he shrieked. 'What is happening? What are you doing to my beautiful school!'

'Oh, you do look a sight, Mr Shrapnell,' said Miss Pandemonium. 'You're covered in bubbles. Don't you worry though. I shall soon have you nice and clean. We can blow them away with the vacuum cleaner.

You stand quite still now, don't move . . .'

Miss Pandemonium switched the vacuum cleaner on to BLOW. The machine roared, whined, coughed and suddenly spat out huge dollops of Friendship Cake. They blasted through the bubbles and thudded against Mr Shrapnell's chest. He staggered back until he hit a wall, then slowly slipped to the floor.

Miss Pandemonium switched off the vacuum cleaner. 'Oh dear. I think there must have been some cake still stuck down the tube Mr Shrapnell. Sorry about that.' She took a cloth and started to wipe the Headmaster's suit clean. 'There you see, it does come off. Mind you, it's left your jacket a bit streaky. Still, it's nice to be different, isn't it? You know, I think we're actually winning our battle, Mr Shrapnell.'

'Battle?' moaned the Head. 'Battle?' It certainly had been a battle. He'd been battling against Miss Pandemonium from the moment she had first set foot in the school.

'Yes, our battle against the cake. There, you're quite clean again.' Miss Pandemonium gave his nose a quick wipe and polish and helped him to his feet. 'Now, shall we go and see what Class Three have been doing?'

Mr Shrapnell hung back. 'I don't think so, no, I can't take any more of this. I just want to go home and sleep.' But Violet Pandemonium had him firmly by the elbow and was guiding him along the corridor.

A few stray bubbles clung to the walls. There was a strong smell of damp carpet and it squelched underfoot, but the

Friendship Cake had gone. The children had steadily pushed it back until it was right outside the building. That was where Mr Shrapnell and Miss Pandemonium found them. They were pouring bucketloads of water over the last smudge of goo, until it had all trickled away down the drains.

'There we are, all gone. Well done everyone, back to class.'

The children smiled at her and hurried off to the classroom, while Miss Pandemonium walked the Head back to his office. He kept mumbling that he didn't understand anything any longer. Miss Pandemonium called to Mrs Bunt and asked her to make the Head a nice strong cup of tea. 'He's had a bit of a shock,' she pointed out.

Once he was in his office Mr Shrapnell

began to recover. Sitting in his old chair –
now nice and clean, though a touch damp
– his head started to clear. Beyond Miss
Pandemonium he could see the school
timetable, still firmly stuck to the wall. The
school timetable! There was his great
strength. Already he could feel it giving
him new life.

He rose to his feet, pushed past Miss
Pandemonium and ran a keen eye over it.
'I knew it! I knew it, Miss Pandemonium.
It doesn't say anything here about cookery.
Mr David's class is never supposed to cook
at all!'

Violet Pandemonium came over and
glanced at the timetable. Mr Shrapnell
pointed out the whole week of work that
was laid out for Class Three, not to
mention all the other classes in the school.
There was even a timetable for Mr

Shrapnell himself. Miss Pandemonium carefully read it through.

'Do you see? NO COOKING!' repeated the Head.

'But how do you manage, Mr Shrapnell?'

'What? What are you going on about now?'

'Your timetable here – it must be so awful for you.' Miss Pandemonium looked at Mr Shrapnell with a childlike expression of wonder. 'Your day is quite full up and you're not allowed one visit to the toilet. How do you know when to go? And what about blowing your nose? How do you manage?'

Mr Shrapnell stared at her. Then he stared at the timetable. He read his own timetable again and again. He stared back at those twinkling grey eyes. Suddenly he was scrabbling at the wall, tearing down the beautiful piece of work, scrumpling it up, shredding it with his bare hands, smashing it with his fists, throwing it to the floor, jumping on it and kicking it violently to all corners of the room.

He stood there, breathing heavily and staring wild-eyed at Miss Pandemonium. At last he opened his mouth.

# 6 Little Things – Big Problems

'Telephone for you, Mr Shrapnell,' called Mrs Bunt. 'I'm putting you through now.'

The Headmaster picked up the receiver and listened. The colour drained from his face. His right eye began to twitch. 'Tomorrow? Tomorrow afternoon? Well, of course, no problem at all. We look forward to seeing you, Mrs Donovan.' He slowly put down the phone. That was it. That must be the last straw. Mrs Donovan was a very important School Inspector, and she was going to visit Dullandon Primary School tomorrow afternoon.

It must mean the end of everything. Mrs Donovan would take one look at Miss Pandemonium and close the entire school.

He'd be sacked, thrown out on his ear after ten years of spotless headship. He walked aimlessly through to Mrs Bunt's office.

'Mrs Bunt? I suppose Miss Pandemonium is here today?'

'Didn't you hear the ambulance, Mr Shrapnell?'

'Yes, yes, though I did try very hard not to. I take it there is no word from Mr David? He won't be in tomorrow?'

'I'm afraid not. The doctor said he mustn't come back to work for at least two weeks.'

Mr Shrapnell nodded brokenly. 'Two weeks,' he muttered. 'Two weeks of Pandemonium.'

'Is there something the matter, Mr Shrapnell?' asked Mrs Bunt.

'No, nothing at all. We only have Mrs

Donovan coming tomorrow afternoon, that's all.'

'Isn't she the Inspector?'

'Yes, the Inspector. The Inspector, Mrs Bunt, but don't let it worry you. I may as well go and stick my head in the gas oven and get it all over with.' He turned away and dragged himself back to his desk. Mrs Bunt watched with interest.

Over in Class Three, Miss Pandemonium had just put an old biscuit tin on her desk.

'What's in there?' asked the class, knowing full well that it could not possibly be biscuits. Miss Pandemonium might carry biscuits in her coat pockets, or at the bottom of her handbag, but never in anything so ordinary as a biscuit tin.

'Mice,' explained Miss Pandemonium. 'You see, my cat is very lazy – he's called

Duvet because he sleeps all day – and he won't catch mice. Unfortunately I've had some mice nibbling away in my kitchen, so I put out some traps for them.'

'Urgh, those aren't dead mice, are they?' muttered Sarah.

'No, I used live traps so I can release them in the wild later. The traps have been out for four nights and when I looked this morning I found I'd caught two wild mice, so I've brought them in to show you. Stuart, I think I saw an old hamster cage out by the sink. See if you can find it.'

Stuart disappeared and a minute later returned with a rather rusty cage. It still had a little exercise wheel inside. Miss Pandemonium opened the top of the cage and took hold of the biscuit tin.

'This is the tricky bit,' she warned. 'Mice are very nervous, so I hope they don't jump out. We don't want them rushing round the class.' She began to prise off the lid, tipping the tin over the cage at the same time. A moment later she gave the tin a shake and two mice slid into the hamster cage. Stuart slammed the lid shut and stood back.

'Well done! That's got them safe and sound.'

'Oh, they're beautiful,' whispered one of the boys.

'Look at that nose,' said Mark. 'It's sniffing. It's all wrinkly.'

'That's because you pong,' Kelly muttered.

'I never knew they were so small,' murmured Jackie.

One of the mice scrambled on to the wheel, which began to squeak and turn. The mouse leaped away as if the wheel had just bitten it. Then it came back, sniffing carefully, and had another go. The children watched, entranced. Miss Pandemonium lifted the cage from her desk.

'I'll put it up here on the shelf where you can all – oh no! Oh dear!'

The cage crashed to the floor as the handle came off in her hands. The door sprang open and the mice were free in an instant. Away they whisked, while half the class threw themselves after them, and the other half stood on their desks yelling.

'They've escaped! They've escaped!'

'It's all right, don't worry,' shouted Miss Pandemonium. 'We'll soon catch them. Where are they now? This way, Kerry! There they are! After them, Amy, quick!'

The mice raced about, twisting and turning as the children tried to close in.

One made a stupendous jump. First it was on a chair, then running across the desktops. That caused even more excitement and the children who were standing there began to dance about as if they were on hot coals.

The second mouse found a cupboard door open and flung itself inside with a little squeak. Four children plunged in after it, scrabbling through books and boxes, rulers, crayons, measuring tapes, puzzles, everything. All of it came flying out behind them as they searched madly for one tiny little creature. It was not long before the cupboard was quite bare. Everything lay in a tip behind them.

'There it is, top shelf! Get it!' squealed Sarah. She jumped up, grabbed the shelf, and a moment later the entire cupboard toppled over on them all.

The door banged and Mr Shrapnell strode into the room. He was greeted by a barrage of yells. 'This way! That way! You go round there!'

Before he could speak Miss Pandemonium had seized him. 'You go that way Mr Shrapnell. There's a mouse loose in the class.'

Mr Shrapnell staggered back as a large cupboard heaved itself from the floor and made straight for him. 'What on earth –!'

'Don't worry, that's Glenn and Rebecca,'

explained Miss Pandemonium. 'Quick – I think it went this way. Look there! Up by the books.'

Mr Shrapnell turned just in time to see a little browny-grey lump whizz across several books and disappear behind them. 'Seen it!' he cried triumphantly, and dived after the little beast. Some of the children cheered. Mr Shrapnell began to shuffle the books, searching behind each one. 'I'm sure it's over here somewhere,' he grunted, as Violet joined him.

She caught sight of the mouse crouching behind an atlas, carefully cupped her hands and moved towards it. The mouse was far too quick. It made a flying leap and scampered right up Mr Shrapnell's jacket sleeve. He never noticed a thing. He was still rummaging through the books.

'Oh, Mr Shrapnell,' said Violet. 'I do believe the mouse has gone up your sleeve.'

'Of course it hasn't. I would have felt it.'

'I'm certain it did. I was just about to capture it when it jumped. It went straight up your sleeve.'

Mr Shrapnell stood up. He looked down at his jacket. He held out his arms, but he couldn't see or feel anything. 'It can't have done,' he repeated.

'It did! It did!' shouted Lyndsey and Cheryl.

'Here, take off your jacket,' suggested Miss Pandemonium, already helping him slip it off. She gave the jacket a shake, but no mouse appeared.

'Are you sure about –'

'There it is, under your jumper!' yelled John. A small tell-tale bulge moved along the bottom of one sleeve. Mr Shrapnell

bent his arm, saw the moving lump and
began a frantic mouse-up-the-sleeve dance.

'Argh! It's got me! Out, out, get out you
horrible little beast!'

He shook his sleeve madly and a
moment later the mouse came leaping
out. As luck would have it, the mouse
fell right into the biscuit tin. Wayne was
there with the lid in an instant before
the mouse could recover.

'Well done, Wayne!' cried Mr Shrapnell.

'Three cheers for Mr Shrapnell!' Lee

shouted. 'Mr Shrapnell caught the mouse
– and Wayne, of course.'

Mr Shrapnell beamed round at
everyone as they cheered. Then the second
mouse was spotted cowering down by the
blackboard. Mr Shrapnell rolled up his
sleeves and put a finger to his lips. A hush
fell upon the children. Flushed with his
recent success the Headmaster carefully
approached the mouse. Bit by bit he got
nearer. The mouse ran forward a little
way. Mr Shrapnell approached from a
different angle. The mouse turned away
and ran until it was trapped in a corner.

The class held its breath as Mr
Shrapnell pressed forward. Now he was
crouching so close he could see every little
tiny hair on its back. His right hand began
to slide ever so slowly towards the creature.
Then, in a flash, his hand shot out,

grabbed the mouse, shoved it in the biscuit tin and slammed on the lid.

Class Three let out its breath and cheered. Mr Shrapnell straightened his tie and looked round the room. Miss Pandemonium was standing at the back smiling and clapping. The Headmaster held up one hand and the noise stopped.

'I think there's a bit of mess that needs clearing up in here, children. Miss Pandemonium, would you mind coming to my office for a moment?'

A wave of fear swept across Class Three and they turned to look at their new teacher. They knew what must happen next. They wished there was something they could do to help. They all felt very small and powerless.

Miss Pandemonium gave a bright smile. 'Of course, Mr Shrapnell. I'm just coming.

Make sure you tidy properly, everyone. I shall be back shortly.'

The Headmaster opened the door for her and she passed through. He frowned back at the children and they hastily began work on clearing up the classroom. Then the door shut, and both of them had gone, leaving the children to their worst fears.

'She'll never be back,' Amber said gloomily.

# 7  An Inspector Calls

'I know what you are going to say, Mr Shrapnell. There are no mice on the timetable.' Miss Pandemonium looked at the Headmaster straight in the eye. He gave her a sharp nod.

'You are quite right, Miss Pandemonium. But you may remember that my timetable was destroyed yesterday afternoon, by myself, after a very, very trying day.'

Violet Pandemonium had to look somewhere else. She found that Mr Shrapnell's expression made her a trifle nervous. He went on.

'There are other copies of the timetable in school of course. However, in the few days that you have been here I have noticed a great deal of excitement among the children. Just forgetting for a moment all the damage and the accidents that have taken place, I have to say that your class has, well – enjoyed themselves. And today, this afternoon . . .' Here Mr Shrapnell took a deep breath, '. . . so did I.'

Mr Shrapnell and Miss Pandemonium gazed at each other. A slow smile came to her face and she gave a little laugh. Mr Shrapnell began to smile too. All at once Miss Pandemonium threw both arms round his neck and planted a plonking kiss on each cheek.

'Oh Mr Shrapnell!' she sighed.

Hastily the Headmaster tried to break away from Miss Pandemonium's giant hug. Just then Mrs Bunt passed by. The school secretary stared at the scene in the Head's office, put a hand to her mouth to stifle a

giggle and ran to her room. Mr Shrapnell finally managed to break Violet's grip.

'Miss Pandemonium! I'm a married man.'

'I know that, Mr Shrapnell, but why shouldn't you hug someone when you're happy? I always hug people when I'm happy. Do you know, sometimes I'm by myself when I'm overcome with joy and I have to hug a tree or a postbox.'

'I can well believe it,' murmured Mr Shrapnell. 'But I haven't quite finished yet. This afternoon I remembered what it is like to really enjoy being at school. I'm sure Class Three have learned a lot over the last few days, but we do have a big problem to face now. Tomorrow afternoon Mrs Donovan, the School Inspector, is coming here. I'm sure I don't need to tell you what that means.'

'Everybody panic?' suggested Miss Pandemonium brightly.

'Yes. That sums it up quite nicely. I think Mr David's class has swimming tomorrow afternoon – that's if you actually do something from the timetetable for once. Well, not much can go wrong with that, I suppose.'

Violet nodded her agreement. 'Don't you worry, Mr Shrapnell. This will be a show school by tomorrow afternoon. I'm really looking forward to using the swimming pool.' She had gone before the

Head could say anything further. Was it his imagination or had she said that last bit in a funny tone of voice, as if she was planning something?

'By the way,' said Miss Pandemonium, suddenly poking her head round the door, 'you wouldn't like my parrot would you? Norman is ever so nice but he keeps trying to nest in my hair – I don't know why. He's quite tame and can make a noise like an ambulance on red alert. You can have him for nothing.' Mr Shrapnell closed his eyes and gravely shook his head. The last thing he wanted was a parrot that did ambulance impressions. The woman was totally mad.

Class Three were amazed to find Miss Pandemonium back at school the next day. 'How did you escape, miss?' asked Wayne.

Miss Pandemonium laughed and said

she would be teaching them until Mr David was well enough to come back to work.

'Oh good!' they cried. 'What are we going to do today then?'

'Well, we've got swimming this afternoon.' Their faces fell.

'All we ever do is go up and down,' complained Julie. 'We're never allowed to dive in or anything. Can't we do something better, miss?'

Violet Pandemonium gazed at the frowning faces, the begging faces and all the fed-up faces in front of her. She gave a little smile. 'Well, what I would like you to do at the pool is split into four groups and find a way of crossing the pool from one side to the other without getting wet.'

'Without getting wet!' Stuart shouted. 'That's impossible.'

Wayne leaped up. 'No it isn't – you could build a boat.'

'Make a bridge,' suggested Sarah.

'We could throw a rope across and swing from it,' Caroline pointed out. 'Me Tarzan!' she added, beating her chest. 'Come on, Cheeta.' She called to Cheryl. 'Let's get to work.'

By the time morning school was over there were four very different answers to the swimming-pool problem. Group One had decided to build a boat using an old tin tub. They had tried to erect a sail but that hadn't worked very well. Instead they had made some oars out of bits of wood.

Group Two had got the metal PE trestles. They planned to throw a rope from one side of the pool to the other. Then they would hang upside down and swarm across.

The third group had also used PE
equipment and were hoping to build a
bridge using the long planks. The last
group had been very busy all morning
making giant floating shoes out of some
large blocks of polystyrene foam they had
found. The idea was to tie these to their
feet and walk across the water.

As soon as lunch was finished the class
grabbed their costumes and carted all the
equipment over to the pool. Miss
Pandemonium said it would be a good

idea to get changed, just in case. She disappeared into one of the cubicles and came out wearing an old striped Victorian swimsuit. She had tried to put on a cap as well, but there was no way any hat would sit on top of her extraordinary hair.

Each group began preparations. There was a large pile of rope, wood, planks, trestles and a tin tub at one side of the pool. They started to lash bits of wood together and measure out rope. They had almost finished this when Mr Shrapnell appeared at the swimming pool with Mrs Donovan, the School Inspector.

Mrs Donovan was a large, red-faced lady with a loud voice and loud make-up. She stared at the jumble stacked by the pool. Her eyes widened with surprise. She blinked several times and then turned to Mr Shrapnell, who was wishing the ground would swallow him up. Couldn't Miss Pandemonium do *anything* right?

'What is going on here?' boomed Mrs Donovan.

Before he could speak, Miss Pandemonium explained.

'We're investigating ways of crossing the pool without getting wet,' she said simply. The Inspector picked up the plans the children had drawn and examined some of the equipment.

'How fascinating,' she murmured, and turned to Julie. 'How are you going to cross the rope once it's in position?'

'I'm going to hang upside down,' Julie replied.

'Oh – like a monkey! What a clever idea! I say, this is fun. What about this one. How does it work?'

'You tie these mini-boats to your feet,' Rebecca said, 'and then walk across – I hope.'

'There are so many good ideas,' said Mrs Donovan. She looked seriously at the children. 'I don't suppose I could have a go at one of them? They look so tempting. I'd love to try the boat.'

Rebecca and Peter giggled and said of course she could have a go. Mrs Donovan put down her handbag and began to clamber into the tub.

'Are you going to try one, Mr Shrapnell?' she called across to the Headmaster.

Mr Shrapnell's jaw dropped. Miss Pandemonium gave him a quick nudge and he jerked back to life. 'Oh, yes, yes, but of course. I'm going to be a monkey,' he announced, much to the delight of Wayne's group. Wayne very kindly said that the Headmaster could have first go.

'Thank you very much,' answered Mr Shrapnell, not at all sure that he wanted to be first.

By this time the tin tub was wobbling crazily across the pool and going really well. Mrs Donovan found it a bit difficult to steer but the most important thing was that it worked. 'This is wonderful!' she shouted back to shore, spinning round and round in small circles.

Mr Shrapnell had thrown aside his jacket and was hauling himself on to the rope. It tensed with his weight. This was a real test. He knew that the whole class was watching. He kicked up his legs and locked both feet over the rope. Then he began to pull himself out over the water.

'Go on, sir! Go on!' shouted the boys. 'You can beat her, sir!'

Mr Shrapnell gritted his teeth and hauled even harder. At this point one of the trestles suddenly gave way under the strain. It slid right into the pool and the Headmaster suddenly found himself floundering about in the water.

'Help!' he yelled, rising spluttering to the surface. He thrashed about madly and grabbed the nearest thing in sight, which happened to be the tin tub, still calmly sailing across the pool. Unfortunately, Mr Shrapnell grabbed it so hard the boat completely overturned and threw the School Inspector into the pool.

'Oh!' cried Mrs Donovan with gurgled surprise. 'Oh! It's wet!' as they both sank beneath the surface.

Half of Class Three threw themselves into the pool to rescue the two adults. Miss Pandemonium raced across to the ambulance and switched on the siren and flashing lights. When she got back there were two very bedraggled adults sitting by the pool, with their clothes clinging to them.

'Are you all right?' asked Violet. Mr Shrapnell coughed, spluttered and asked

her to please switch off that awful noise.

The School Inspector wrung out her
sleeves and turned to him.

'Mr Shrapnell, I haven't enjoyed a
school visit so much for ages. I have to
say I am delighted at the change at
Dullandon. I used to hate coming here. It
was always so stuffy with that wretched
timetable of yours. Of course, timetables
are useful and necessary, but you can go

over the top. As for this class, it is a credit to the school. I can assure you I shall be making a very good report. Now I had better go and get dry somehow.'

Mrs Donovan squelched off to a changing room. Mr Shrapnell watched her go. Then he began to laugh. The children started to laugh. Miss Pandemonium started to laugh. Mr Shrapnell got to his feet and carefully got into the tin tub. He took up an oar.

'May I row you round the pool, Violet?' he asked.

'I'd be delighted, Headmaster,' smiled Miss Pandemonium. She climbed into the tub and they began to paddle sedately round the pool while the children cheered and waved.

And even as the tub began to sink lower and lower with their weight they

didn't care, and slowly slid beneath the

waves, laughing.

# It all started with a Scarecrow.

**Puffin is seventy years old.**
Sounds ancient, doesn't it? But Puffin has never been
so lively. We're always on the lookout for the next big
idea, which is how it began all those years ago.

Penguin Books was a big idea from the mind of
a man called Allen Lane, who in 1935 invented
the quality paperback and changed the world.
**And from great Penguins, great Puffins grew,
changing the face of children's books forever.**

The first four Puffin Picture Books were hatched in 1940 and the
first Puffin story book featured a man with broomstick arms called
Worzel Gummidge. In 1967 Kaye Webb, Puffin Editor, started the
Puffin Club, promising to 'make children into readers'.
She kept that promise and over 200,000 children became
devoted Puffineers through their quarterly instalments of
*Puffin Post*, which is now back for a new generation.

Many years from now, we hope you'll look back and
remember Puffin with a smile. **No matter what your age
or what you're into, there's a Puffin for everyone.**
The possibilities are endless, but one thing is for sure:
whether it's a picture book or a paperback, a sticker book
or a hardback, **if it's got that little Puffin
on it – it's bound to be good.**

## JOKE BOOKS
You'll never be stuck for a
joke to share again.

## THE HUNDRED-MILE-AN-HOUR DOG
Streaker is no ordinary dog; she's a rocket on
four legs with a woof attached . . .

## COSMIC PYJAMAS
Pyjamas are just pyjamas, right?
Not when they're COSMIC
PYJAMAS, swooooosh! . . .

## COWS, CARTOONS, ALIENS AND . . . ORANG-UTANS?!
Warning - may induce red cheeks and tears of laughter!

# LAUGH YOUR Socks off with Jeremy STRONG

Jeremy Strong has written SO many books to make you laugh your socks right off. There are the Streaker books and the Famous Bottom books and the Pyjamas books and ... PHEW!

Welcome to the JEREMY STRONG FAMILY TREE, which shows you all of Jeremy's brilliant books in one easy-to-follow-while-laughing-your-socks-off way!

## MY BROTHER'S FAMOUS BOTTOM

Nicholas's baby brother, Cheese, is famous. Well, his bottom is, because he advertises Dumper disposable nappies ...

Pirate Pandemonium

PUFFIN BOOKS

Jeremy Strong once worked in a bakery, putting the jam into three thousand doughnuts every night. Now he puts the jam in stories instead, which he finds much more exciting. At the age of three, he fell out of a first-floor bedroom window and landed on his head. His mother says that this damaged him for the rest of his life and refuses to take any responsibility. He loves writing stories because he says it is 'the only time you alone have complete control and can make anything happen'. His ambition is to make you laugh (or at least snuffle). Jeremy Strong lives near Bath with his wife, Gillie, four cats and a flying cow.

*Are you feeling silly enough to read more?*

LAUGH YOUR SOCKS OFF WITH

# Jeremy STRONG

# Pirate Pandemonium

Illustrated by

## Judy Brown

PUFFIN

*For Jane, and anarchy and imagination*
*in the classroom*

PUFFIN BOOKS

Published by the Penguin Group
Penguin Books Ltd, 80 Strand, London WC2R ORL, England
Penguin Group (USA) Inc., 375 Hudson Street, New York, New York 10014, USA
Penguin Group (Canada), 90 Eglinton Avenue East, Suite 700, Toronto, Ontario, Canada M4P 2Y3
(a division of Pearson Penguin Canada Inc.)
Penguin Ireland, 25 St Stephen's Green, Dublin 2, Ireland (a division of Penguin Books Ltd)
Penguin Group (Australia), 250 Camberwell Road, Camberwell, Victoria 3124, Australia
(a division of Pearson Australia Group Pty Ltd)
Penguin Books India Pvt Ltd, 11 Community Centre, Panchsheel Park, New Delhi – 110 017, India
Penguin Group (NZ), 67 Apollo Drive, Rosedale, Auckland 0632, New Zealand
(a division of Pearson New Zealand Ltd)
Penguin Books (South Africa) (Pty) Ltd, 24 Sturdee Avenue, Rosebank, Johannesburg 2196, South Africa

Penguin Books Ltd, Registered Offices: 80 Strand, London WC2R ORL, England

puffinbooks.com

First published by A & C Black (Publishers) Ltd 1997
First published in Puffin Books 1999
Published in this edition 2011
001 – 10 9 8 7 6 5 4 3 2 1

Text copyright © Jeremy Strong, 1997
Illustrations copyright © Judy Brown, 1997
All rights reserved

The moral right of the author and illustrator has been asserted

Set in Baskerville MT
Made and printed in Great Britain by Clays Ltd, St Ives plc

Except in the United States of America, this book is sold subject to the condition
that it shall not, by way of trade or otherwise, be lent, re-sold, hired out, or otherwise
circulated without the publisher's prior consent in any form of binding or cover other than
that in which it is published and without a similar condition including this condition
being imposed on the subsequent purchaser

British Library Cataloguing in Publication Data
A CIP catalogue record for this book is available from the British Library

ISBN: 978–0–141–33617–6

www.greenpenguin.co.uk

MIX
Paper from
responsible sources
FSC
www.fsc.org   FSC™ C018179

Penguin Books is committed to a sustainable
future for our business, our readers and our
planet. This book is made from paper certified
by the Forest Stewardship Council.

# Contents

# 1 A Telephone Call

It was a rather strange shape. It was
meant to be a clay elephant, but it looked
more like the result of a high-speed, head-
on collision between an octopus and a
hippopotamus. Violet Pandemonium had
only recently taken up pottery. She had
been getting rather bored and needed
something to do. Normally she had
plenty of work as a supply teacher, but
recently not a single school had
telephoned her to ask if she would like to
come and look after a class because the
teacher was ill. Miss Pandemonium could
not understand it. 'Perhaps the
government has banned teachers from
being ill,' she wondered.

Then one day she noticed in the local

newspaper that someone was selling:

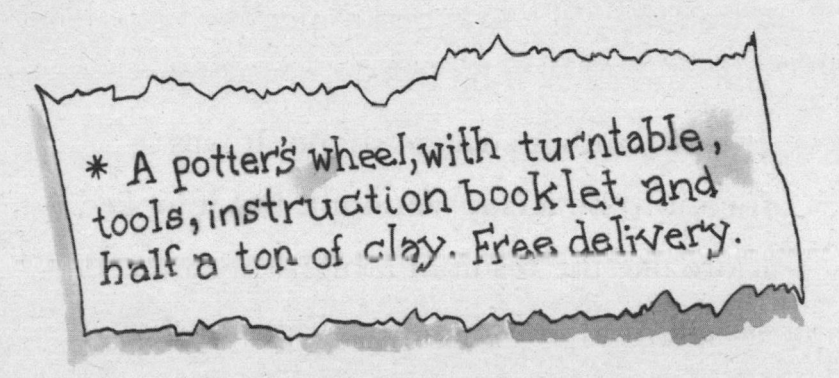

* A potter's wheel, with turntable, tools, instruction booklet and half a ton of clay. Free delivery.

Miss Pandemonium thought it sounded like a chance not to be missed. 'I've always fancied going potty,' she giggled, and rang up immediately and bought the lot.

Violet had not realized how much half a ton of clay was. She lived in a small house in the middle of a terrace, with no front garden and, being rather short of space, she had to put the clay in her bath, where it sat like some hideous misshapen life-form. Excitedly, she set up the potter's wheel at once, put her foot on the treadle

and soon had the wheel spinning round at a fine rate. She grabbed a nice big blob of clay and stuck it on the wheel. Much to her surprise the clay was immediately flung off at high speed. Violet watched as it whizzed across the room and splattered across Auntie Dora's face. Fortunately it was only a photograph of Auntie Dora.

Miss P. cleaned up Auntie as best she could, blew her a kiss by way of an apology and had another try. The second

blob of clay did much the same thing, except that it flew off in a different direction, zoomed out through the open window and hit a passing cyclist. It flopped over his head like a big brown pancake.

Unable to see where he was going, the cyclist rode straight up a plank and into the back of a builder's van. When the builder went to his van to get some bricks he found a dazed cyclist with something like a cowpat sitting on his head, trying to untangle himself from the remains of his twisted bike.

As for Violet Pandemonium, she had no idea what had happened. She was still searching round her front room, wondering where the clay missile had gone. The potter's wheel was proving to be a little unpredictable, so Miss P. decided to try some modelling with her hands

instead. That was when she made the elephant – or was it a hippopoctopus?

She was just putting the finishing touches to it when the telephone rang. Miss Pandemonium jumped up to answer it. 'Hello . . . yes, I'm Miss Pandemonium, at least I was when I got up this morning . . . oh! . . . straight away? Well yes, I can. Which school is it? Witts End Primary . . . a class of nine- and ten-year-olds . . . yes, that's fine . . . I shall be with you in half an hour . . . bye-eee!'

Miss P. tried to put the phone down, but her hands were covered in wet clay and the telephone stuck to her as if it had been glued to her fingers. She pulled the phone from her right hand with her left and the phone stuck to her left hand instead. After several minutes, she eventually managed to escape by pushing the phone out of her

hand with one elbow. She had clay halfway up both arms, and the phone was now attached to her left elbow. She shook it off, rushed to the kitchen, had a good wash and then set about getting ready for school.

Miss Pandemonium quickly stuffed a multitude of bits and bobs into a big canvas holdall. 'Now, let's see, have I got everything? Have I got my bag of teaching gear? Yes. Have I got my lunch? No. I shall have to have a school lunch today. Have I got my First Aid bag, my

Medical Encyclopaedia and Emergency Acupuncture Kit? Yes. Have I got my glasses? No – don't be silly, Violet, you don't wear glasses. OK, let's go!'

Miss Pandemonium rushed out through the front door, dropped a bag, picked it up, leapt into her second-hand ambulance and set off for Witts End Primary School with all lights flashing and the siren wailing.

It was astonishing how empty the roads were when Miss Pandemonium went out in her ambulance. Cars hastily pulled over to one side. Lorries stopped dead. Even the police cheerily waved her on, thinking there was a major emergency somewhere. Miss P. had a clear and easy drive to the school. With a haul on the steering wheel she skidded into the Witts Ends School car park, siren still blaring, found a parking space, did a five-point turn with gears

crunching, screeched to a halt and jumped out.

'Oh!' said Miss Pandemonium as she turned to go into the school. 'A welcoming committee – how nice!' Peering from every window were faces – children's faces, teachers' faces, cooks' faces, the secretary, the caretaker, and the head teacher. Everyone had heard the siren. Everyone

had seen the ambulance arrive. Now they could all see Miss Pandemonium too.

Mr Kuddle, the head teacher, hurried across the car park to meet her, stooping to pick up her bags as she dropped them one by one. 'So glad you're here,' he began, retrieving bag number one. 'I'm Mr Kuddle. I'm the head. You can call me Kevin – everybody does – well, to my face anyway, ha ha! Who knows what they call me behind my back! Ha ha! Lovely ambulance – lovely. Mrs Colon – she has Class Five usually – she's got a bit of a tummy problem and won't be back for two weeks or so. Nice class, Class Five – got some characters in there, I can tell you, ha ha! Be firm but kind, that's what I say. We must earn their respect. That's Class Five over there, the ones that are waving and shouting at us – oh look, I think Samantha

Boggis has just thrown Gary out of the window. Never mind, he's used to it. He knows his way back. Lovely girl, Samantha – bags of character. Well, good luck, Miss um, Miss um-mum . . .?'

'Pandemonium,' smiled Miss P., who was at last able to get a word in. 'But call me Violet.'

'Kevin,' nodded Mr Kuddle.

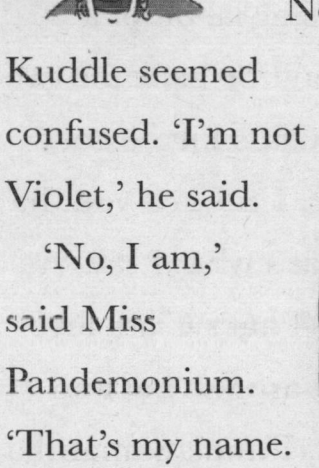

Miss Pandemonium frowned slightly.

'No, not Kevin, Violet.'

Now Mr

Kuddle seemed confused. 'I'm not Violet,' he said.

'No, I am,' said Miss Pandemonium. 'That's my name.

Why did you call me Kevin?'

'Did I? How odd. Kevin is my name.'

They both stopped by the main entrance. 'So I'm Kevin and you're Violet,' repeated Mr Kuddle, and his bushy moustache gave a cheerful wriggle. 'Good, ha ha! Class Five is up the corridor, last door on the left. Lovely children, lovely. High-spirited little lot! We have a busy time ahead – it's Book Week, you know, and we are having a new school library opened on Friday by the Mayor. Each class is choosing a special book topic and everybody's going to dress up. Thought I'd come as Robocop, ha ha! Oh well, see you later um, Violin.'

Before Miss Pandemonium could correct him, he had gone scurrying back to his little office and shutting the door quickly behind him. Miss Pandemonium

grasped her bags
firmly and set off
down the long
corridor.

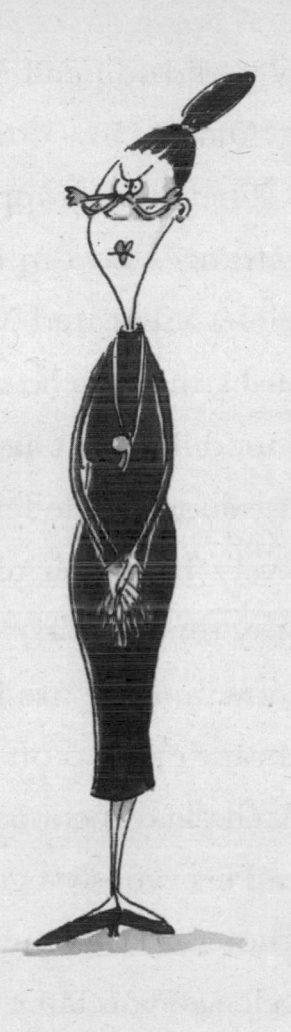

Halfway down the
corridor a classroom
door suddenly flew
open and a striking
figure appeared. A
tall, thin, elderly lady
stood framed in the
doorway. She was
wearing what
looked like a long
black evening
dress, and she
stood there, posed like an ancient
model, with her raven-black hair piled up
on her head in an enormous beehive
hairdo. She whipped off her vulture-like

glasses and fixed Violet with a penetrating glare.

'Mrs Earwigger,' she announced curtly. 'Deputy head. You're in the room next door. No noise. Thank you.' And with that she gave a brief nod and vanished back into her classroom.

Violet Pandemonium put down her bags and stared in surprise at the shut door. She went across to it, pulled the door open, poked her cheerful face round the frame and smiled in at Mrs Earwigger, who appeared most shocked that anyone had opened her door at all, especially without knocking. After all, nobody ever dared to go anywhere near her room.

A sea of curious little faces gazed back at Miss Pandemonium. A visitor! They never had visitors! Visitors to Mrs Earwigger's class were like aliens from a distant planet.

Violet smiled across at the astonished
deputy head.

'Violet Pandemonium,' she announced.
'Supply teacher. I'm in the class next door.
Loads of noise. I've come to teach them
how to tap dance and play the drums.
Bye-eee.' And with that she closed the
door, picked up her bags and went.

Inside Mrs Earwigger's classroom you
could have heard a pin drop. Mrs
Earwigger stared at the classroom door as

if it had just stuck out its tongue at her and burped, very loudly. The children stared at Mrs Earwigger, wondering what she would do next, glancing at each other, with tiny smiles hiding on their lips.

Then Mrs Earwigger's mouth began to do something very strange. The children didn't find it strange at all, because Mrs Earwigger's mouth was famous for doing exactly this. In fact, the children often tried to copy it in the playground, but nobody did it as well as Mrs Earwigger herself.

Her mouth began to scrunch up. It sucked itself inwards, so that her

thin lips puckered up into a mass of wrinkles, and finally her mouth disappeared, just as if she had swallowed it. This is what Mrs Earwigger did when she was totally flabbergasted. Other people might shout, scream, pull their hair and jump up and down, but Mrs Earwigger sucked up her mouth until it vanished.

Miss Pandemonium had arrived, and nothing and nobody at Witts End Primary School would ever be quite the same.

# 2  Introducing Class Five – Beware!

Miss Pandemonium pushed open the door of Class Five and walked in. She was used to being greeted by a huddle of children with expectant faces, sitting quietly at their tables. But Class Five was different. They were not in a huddle, they were not quiet and they were not looking the least bit expectant either.

Samantha Boggis was busy throwing Gary out of a window for the fifth time that morning. A large group of children at the back of the class appeared to be having an 'Everybody-Welcome-to-Wrestling' competition. And a section of Samantha Boggis's all-girl gang had captured three boys and sentenced them to a life of slavery.

'Good morning, everyone!' cried Miss Pandemonium cheerfully. She was completely ignored. Violet watched them for a few moments. 'I see,' she muttered to herself, and dived into her enormous hold-all. First of all she pulled out a small, portable electric cooker, put it on her desk and plugged it into a wall socket. Then she went back to the bag and got out a large empty tin can, with a screw top.

The bunch of wrestlers stopped tying each other into knots and sat down to watch the strange woman doing even stranger things with a tin can. Violet took the empty can to the sink and poured a little cold water into it. Then she took the can back to her desk and placed it on the cooker. While the water was coming to the boil Violet set about cleaning the blackboard, which was covered with remarks like:

'Tom Nunnery stinks'

'Tracey loves Mike'

'Darren Oates has pimples on his b —'

(The rest was smeared.)

Miss Pandemonium appeared to completely ignore the children, most of whom had now slipped quietly back to their tables and had their eyes glued to the tin can on the cooker. Steam was spouting up from the little hole in the top.

'It's boiling, miss,' said Darren.

'Oh! So it is.' Miss Pandemonium turned from the clean blackboard, switched off the cooker and removed the can from the heat. She picked up the screw top and carefully screwed the lid on to the can. Then she put it on her desk and without a word began to unpack some of her bits and pieces. Even Samantha Boggis and her gang now had their eyes fixed on the can. What on earth was this weird woman doing?

Nothing happened, and then, just as Class Five were beginning to get restless

once again, there was a
loud CLUNK, and
one wall of the tin
can bent inwards.

This was quickly
followed by another
loud CLANG, and
the whole tin doubled
over, as if it had been

punched in the belly by a gigantic
invisible fist.

There was one more ear-splitting
SCRANG, and the tin completely
collapsed in upon
itself, toppled
over and crashed
to the floor.

Class Five rose to
their feet and stared down at

the crumpled can. Then they looked at each other with bewildered faces. 'How did that happen?' demanded Samantha. 'How did you do that?'

'Air pressure,' answered Miss Pandemonium. 'Steam drove the air from the can, so that when I put the lid on there was less air inside the can than there was outside it. That meant there was more air pressure outside than there was inside, so the can was crushed by air pressure.'

'Do it again!' cried Mike.

'Bring me a can tomorrow and I'll do it again,' smiled Violet. Tracey frowned.

'Are you here tomorrow then?'

'Yes. I'm here until Mrs Colon gets better.'

'That's what Mrs Earwigger does,' a voice said quietly from the back of the

class. Everyone turned round and glared at a small, freckled boy.

'Oh shut up, Gary!' they cried.

'But she does,' insisted Gary. 'It must be air pressure. When she gets all cross and steamy she shuts her mouth and then it all sucks in on itself, just like that tin can. I bet it's air pressure.'

'Gary,' said Samantha threateningly, 'if you open your mouth once more I'm going to stuff your plimsoll bag inside it.'

'Oh, I don't think so,' said Mrs Pandemonium. 'We have far more important things to do. I hear it's Book Week this week, and everybody is going to dress up. Mr Kuddle told me that each class is choosing a special topic. Have you chosen one yet?'

After several grunts and grumbles Michelle explained that nobody was ever

allowed to choose a theme for Book Week because Mrs Earwigger always decided what everyone was going to do.

'I see,' murmured Miss Pandemonium. 'Mrs Earwigger decides what every class will do, not just her own class?' The children nodded glumly. 'What would happen if we chose a topic for ourselves?' asked Violet.

Eyes began to boggle. Jaws dropped. Eyebrows shot all over the place, and there

was a severe outbreak of spine-chilling goosepimples.

There was such an air of excited, scared astonishment that Miss Pandemonium got the impression that such a thing had never been heard of before. She asked the class if Mrs Earwigger had chosen a topic for Class Five yet.

'Yes,' said Ryan. 'Flower Fairies. Mrs Earwigger has got a Flower Fairies Address Book, and it's her most favourite book and she wants everyone in Class Five to dress up as a Flower Fairy.' For some reason Ryan didn't sound too enthusiastic about the idea.

'Yes, that sounds very interesting,' said Miss Pandemonium, who wasn't at all sure that Book Weeks were meant to celebrate address books. 'And are you all looking forward to being Flower Fairies?'

This question produced an explosion of answers. 'In that case,' said Miss Pandemonium, 'we had better think of something else. How about Winnie-the-Pooh?'

'Winnie-the-Pooh stinks,' muttered Tony, much to everyone's amusement.

'Robinson Crusoe?' Miss Pandemonium offered.

'There's only one Robinson Crusoe,' Cleo pointed out. 'We can't all be Robinson Crusoe.'

'Very true,' murmured Miss P. 'All right, what about Peter Pan?'

'There are fairies in Peter Pan,' grumbled James, 'and loads of goody-goodies.'

'Yeah, but there's Captain Hook and his pirates,' said Samantha. 'I could be Captain Hook.'

'You're a girl!' yelled Darren. 'Girls can't be pirate captains!'

'Who says!' screeched Samantha, jumping to her feet and fixing Darren with a murderous stare.

'Why don't we all be pirates?' said Miss Pandemonium calmly. 'We don't have to do Peter Pan at all. We can do a class topic on pirates and then everyone can be a pirate.'

This last suggestion seemed to go down pretty well, until Tom said that girls couldn't be pirates because girls were too girly and didn't know how to hold a sword properly and could never kill anyone because they'd be too busy wanting to be nurses instead. 'They'd stick their sword in someone and then say, "Oh, terribly sorry, have I made you bleed? Here, let me bandage it up for you".'

The boys roared with laughter, until Samantha stood on her chair and glared at them furiously. 'I bet girls make much better pirates than boys,' she shouted, daring the boys to say otherwise. Darren and Wayne needed no encouragement. They leapt from their tables, brandishing their rulers fiercely. 'Come on then, prove it!' they challenged. Within seconds there was a full-scale battle between the boys on one side and the girls on the other. Rulers flashed in the sunlight, fierce faces growled and gnashed their teeth, while Miss Pandemonium seized a metre ruler and stood on her desk, urging the girls on to

victory, waving her metre-sword round her head and bashing the light fittings several times as she did so.

'Charge!' screamed Samantha, hurling herself across the classroom.

'Stand by to repel boarders!' roared Mike.

Just as the fight reached fever pitch, the
door opened and Mrs Earwigger marched
straight in, blowing a shrill whistle.
Everyone stopped and looked at the
deputy head. Mrs Earwigger glared up at
Miss Pandemonium.

'What on earth is going on in here?'
demanded Mrs Earwigger.

'We were trying to decide if women
pirates are better than men pirates,' Miss

Pandemonium explained, as she struggled to replace one of the light fittings she had knocked down. 'I think it was pretty even actually. What do you think, Mrs Earwigger?'

'What do I think? I have never heard anything like it in my life.'

'You've never heard pirates fighting before?' asked Miss Pandemonium.

'No, of course not! I mean, it's ridiculous. And you – you're standing on your desk.'

'Yes?'

'Teachers don't stand on their desks in this school!' snapped the deputy.

'Oh. Why's that?' asked Miss Pandemonium innocently. 'You see, this is the quarterdeck really. I was standing on the quarterdeck to get a better view of my pirate crew.'

'Your pirate crew!'

'Yes. We've decided to be pirates for Book Week. That's our topic.'

'But you can't. You're a Flower Fairy. You're all Flower Fairies.' Mrs Earwigger was beside herself.

'Not any more,' Miss Pandemonium explained. 'We've decided we prefer being pirates, haven't we, children?'

The astonished children nodded dumbly. Mrs Earwigger was totally gobsmacked. She drew in her breath sharply, closed her mouth and began her party trick.

'Air pressure,' hissed Gary. 'You watch.' And everyone did, as Mrs Earwigger's mouth crumpled up and all of a sudden vanished. The deputy head stalked out of the room and slammed the door shut. There was a sigh of relief from the

children and they went back to their chairs.

'You're in trouble now, miss,' said Samantha, with some admiration.

'Why, what have I done?'

'You've changed her Book Week plan. We're going to be pirates and that's going to be much better than what Class Six are going to be. Nobody's supposed to be better than Class Six because it's Mrs Earwigger's class and they're always the best. Nobody has ever changed what Mrs Earwigger says, and you answered back to her.'

'You're not supposed to answer back,' explained Kimberley. 'You're just supposed to listen. Even Mr Kuddle doesn't answer back to Mrs Earwigger.'

'Really? How strange. Tell me, what is Class Six's topic?'

'Roman Gods and Goddesses,' announced Dawn. 'Class Six do Gods and Goddesses every time we dress up for Book Week. They come as Jupiter and Venus and Mars and all that lot. Then they all stand around looking very snooty and they order everyone about.'

'I see,' murmured Miss Pandemonium. 'I must admit that Gods and Goddesses doesn't sound terribly exciting. Well, I think we had better get on with our topic. I guess we have proved that girls can be good pirates too and in fact there used to be quite a lot of famous women pirates that sailed the seven seas.'

'Is that true, miss?' asked Samantha, who was just as amazed to hear this as everyone else.

'Oh yes,' said Miss Pandemonium. 'Several of them ended up walking the

plank, just like the men pirates.'

'Can we do walking the plank as well, miss?' asked Wayne. 'I'd like to be in charge of that.'

'Maybe we'll leave that till a bit later. What we need to do first is find out about pirates — how they lived, how they dressed and so on, so that we get some ideas for what we want to wear and what we are going to do.'

There was an immediate rush to the book shelves in the classroom to see what could be discovered about pirates, and Miss Pandemonium settled down to a peaceful morning. As the children started to collect the information they needed Miss Pandemonium turned her thoughts to the deputy head. What a strange woman Mrs Earwigger was, and why did everyone do what she said all the time?

# 3  Battle Commences

Mrs Earwigger stood in Mr Kuddle's little office glaring down her nose at the head teacher. Mr Kuddle sat hunched at his desk, looking distinctly uncomfortable. It was  a big desk and he was very fond of it – when he sat on the far side it was difficult for anyone to get near him, especially Mrs Earwigger. Mr Kuddle spent a lot of his time making sure that there was as much distance between himself and Mrs Earwigger as possible.

'She was standing on her table, Mr Kuddle,' snapped the deputy head. 'The children were fighting and this . . . woman . . . was encouraging them. Now, what are we going to do about it?'

'This is Miss Pandemonium's first day here,' began Mr Kuddle. 'I think we should all be friends. A friendly school is a happy school.'

'Mr Kuddle, Class Five were practising at being pirates,' explained Mrs Earwigger. The head teacher mumbled something about pirates being very appropriate for Class Five, but luckily the deputy didn't hear him. 'What is more,' she continued, 'Class Five are going to be pirates for the whole of Book Week.'

'Good idea.'

'It is not a good idea at all, Mr Kuddle,' snapped Mrs Earwigger. 'If you remember,

'I have already decided what everyone will be for our Book Week. Mrs Patel is going to be Snow White and her four-year-olds are going to be the seven dwarfs.'

'But there are twenty-seven children in Mrs Patel's reception class, not seven.'

'I am well aware of that, Mr Kuddle, but they are the only children small enough to be dwarfs,' Mrs Earwigger pointed out with flawless logic.

'Mrs Patel is not exactly, er . . .' Poor Mr Kuddle struggled to find the right words.

'I agree that Mrs Patel is not ideal for Snow White. She is rather large and fifty-three years old, but I'm sure her little dwarfs won't mind.'

Mr Kuddle wasn't so sure about this, but he didn't have the courage to pursue it further. 'What about Class Two?' he sighed.

'Noddy and the Toyland folk,' said his deputy cheerfully, and she carried on with her list. 'Class Three are going to be rabbits.'

'Rabbits? All of them?'

'Yes, you know, Flopsy, Mopsy, Popsy, Wopsy, Topsy, Bopsy, Slopsy, Chopsy . . . all those rabbits that Beatrix Potter wrote about.'

'I'm not sure there was a Popsy,' began Mr Kuddle, 'or a Slopsy, or a Topsy for that matter.'

'There's no point in getting picky about it, Mr Kuddle. Class Three are all going to be rabbits. Besides, we're getting off the point. The reason I am here is because Miss Pandemonium has told Class Five

they can be pirates, and it doesn't fit in with my Book Week plans at all, so what are you going to do about it?'

The head teacher tugged nervously at his big moustache. 'Let's give Miss Pandemonium a day or two to settle in. Remember that she has got Class Five, and they are a difficult bunch.'

'I'm sure I'd have no difficulties with them,' snapped the deputy.

'No,' agreed Mr Kuddle, thinking that Mrs Earwigger wouldn't have any difficulty wrestling Jaws with her bare hands. 'But Miss Pandemonium has only just arrived at the school and she is helping us out until Mrs Colon comes back.' Mr Kuddle suddenly felt rather brave. 'I say we let the children be pirates.'

Mrs Earwigger stared at the head teacher. She couldn't believe her ears. Mr

Kuddle was actually daring to oppose her. He had never opposed her in all the five years that he had been head. It was all that wretched woman's doing: Miss Pandemonium had a lot to answer for.

'You are going to allow Class Five to be pirates?'

Mr Kuddle swallowed hard and nodded, trying to avoid the spear-like glare that Mrs Earwigger had stabbed him with.

'You will let them run riot all over the school, causing mayhem and injury?'

'I don't think it will be like that,' murmured Mr Kuddle, desperately hoping that it wouldn't. 'I'm quite sure that Miss Pandemonium will have everything under control.'

'On your head be it,' snapped the deputy, and she stalked out, slamming the door. Mr Kuddle closed his eyes and began

to plan his next summer holiday.
Would South America be far
enough away?

Mrs Earwigger
stood outside the door
for a moment,
recovering her composure. She
patted her black beehive so that it
stood straight and tall. Her eyes
narrowed until they
were thin,
determined
slits. There was
no way she was
going to have all
her plans changed by
a mere supply teacher like Miss
Pandemonium. Oh no, that woman was in
for a very nasty shock.

*

By the middle of the afternoon, Class
Five were deep into pirate lore and had
begun collecting ideas for what kind of
pirates they wanted to be. Wayne was
so taken with having a black eyepatch
that he decided he was going to wear
two.

'Don't be stupid,' Cleo snorted. 'If you
wear two you'll be blind.'

'So? I can be a blind pirate if I want to.'
But even Wayne didn't sound too
convinced.

'It says here that pirates often kept pets
on board ship,' Michelle called out. 'I'm
going to be a pirate with a pet.'

'You've only got a stick insect at home,'
shouted James. 'How can you be a pirate
with a stick insect?'

'Yeah, but my uncle's got a monkey and
I'm going to bring that in.'

'Your uncle's never got a monkey!'
James was distinctly jealous.

'Has, so there.'

'Well, he'll never let you bring it in,' said
James, but Michelle just smiled at him and
stuck out her tongue.

'Are you going to be a pirate, miss?'
Darren asked Miss Pandemonium.

'Oh yes. I've already decided who I'm
going to be, I shall be Captain
Blackbeard.'

'Oh! We thought you'd be a woman
pirate.'

'I could be, but I've always fancied being
Blackbeard. He had a long, wild black
hair, and he used to tie gunpowder fuses
into it and light them before he leapt on to
the enemy ship. He must have looked
terrifying.'

'Sounds a bit like Mrs Earwigger,'

muttered Jennifer, and everyone laughed.

'Can we have a boat?' Gary suddenly asked.

'Gary!' the whole class chorused. 'You're so stupid!'

But Miss Pandemonium thought it was an excellent suggestion. 'We can't have a real boat, but why don't we turn this classroom into our pirate galleon? Look, the windows down the side can be our gun-ports . . .'

'Yeah – brilliant! We can make cannons and stick them out of the window and shoot everyone,' cried Stewart.

'And we can make prisoners walk the plank,' hissed Samantha Boggis, looking directly at the hapless Gary. 'I'm going to enjoy this.'

Miss Pandemonium gazed at the sea of happy, interested faces. This was going to

be a lovely week, she thought. Little did
she realize just what Class Five would get
up to – let alone Class Six. Class Six was
the top class, the oldest class, and it was
Mrs Earwigger's class. Nobody
was allowed to teach Year
Six children except Mrs
Earwigger. This could
have been because Mrs
Earwigger didn't like little
children who needed their
laces tying and their noses

wiped; who couldn't hold scissors properly and had a habit of being sick in the sand tray.

It could have been because the youngest children knew the least, so they needed the most teaching. It could also have been because teaching Year Six children was, compared to meeting the demands of the very young, quite an easy life. Or it could have been, as Mrs Earwigger always claimed, that Year Six were the most demanding children who required the finest teaching possible — in other words hers.

Class Six were not looking forward to Book Week. They knew exactly what to expect, and when Mrs Earwigger told them they could all come as Roman Gods and Goddesses they just gazed glumly at each other. She pinned a list next to the

blackboard from which the children could choose such delightfully interesting characters as Cupid, Aurora, Mercury and so on.

Class Six were so excited by this that they couldn't even speak and, eventually, when one boy did manage to say something it sounded surprisingly like a groan of despair.

Mrs Earwigger spent the whole lunch hour and half the afternoon with her brain in a whirl. It was as if all the bees in her beehive hairdo had escaped into her brain,

and there they buzzed, menacingly. What could she do to outsmart that wretched Miss Pandemonium? If Class Five dressed up as pirates they would steal the show. The whole point of giving stupid topics to the other classes was so that Class Six, her class, would appear wonderful. If only she had thought of letting Class Six be pirates. Pirates? It was monstrous!

By the time the end of the day arrived, Mrs Earwigger was still seething – she still hadn't come up with a plan that would put Miss Pandemonium in her place. The deputy head sent

the children home in a fit of bad temper –
not that they noticed, she seemed the same
as usual to them – and spent the whole
evening racking her brains for a solution.

# 4 Give Us Your Treasure!

A distant wail could be heard, rapidly approaching the school. 'It's Miss Pandemonium,' said Gary, and he was right. Violet's ambulance skidded into the car park and screeched to a halt. She jumped out, dropped half her bags, and skipped across the playground towards Class Five. The children watched from the windows.

'Do you think she's mad?' wondered Tina.

'I don't care,' Ryan said. 'She's changed The Earwig's plans, and I reckon she deserves a medal for bravery.'

The classroom door burst open and Miss Pandemonium rushed in, spilling the contents of one bag across the floor and

knocking six plants from their tray before
finally reaching her desk.

'Sorry I'm late,' she cried, 'but my
hamster got sucked up by the vacuum
cleaner. I switched to BLOW, and the poor
thing shot back out and landed in my bowl
of cornflakes. I had to take him to the
bathroom for a shampoo and blow-dry.
He's all right now, thank goodness, but I
think he's gone off cornflakes.'

'She *is* mad,' whispered Tracey to
Samantha.

'Is Michelle here yet?' asked Violet, smiling cheerfully at everyone.

'Over here, miss.'

'Did you get your uncle's monkey?' asked Miss Pandemonium.

'No, miss, he was out.' This was greeted by a roar from James.

'I said you didn't have a monkey. I said you wouldn't bring it in.'

'I do! I will! You see if I don't! I can't help it if my uncle was out.'

'Yeah? I bet you haven't even got an uncle, let alone a monkey.'

'James! Michelle!' cried Violet. 'I don't want to hear any more about it. The monkey isn't here today and that's fine. Perhaps you will be able to get hold of it for tomorrow, Michelle? It can join in the Fancy Dress fun.'

'I'll try, miss.'

Class Five settled down while Miss Pandemonium sorted out the register, and then they asked what they were going to do all day. Violet gazed at their expectant faces. 'Well, I thought we should spend the day getting into the spirit of being pirates, ready for tomorrow. You know what pirates used to do, don't you?'

'Kill people!' shouted Samantha Boggis. 'Can we kill Class Six, please, miss?'

'Not this week, Samantha, if you don't mind, and certainly not while I'm here. Pirates did a lot of kidnapping and marooning and holding people to ransom. They used to board ships and seize all their gold and jewels and then they'd sail off to secret islands and bury their ill-gotten gains.'

'Sounds good to me,' grinned Samantha.

'In my ambulance I have some bits and pieces that might be useful to us,' Miss Pandemonium went on. 'If we are going to turn this classroom into a pirate galleon we shall need swords and daggers, and cannons and cannon balls. We also need some treasure, and I thought we could make a few raids, like real pirates.'

Samantha Boggis could hardly believe her luck. 'Raids, miss? Real raids – I mean waving swords and threatening people and stealing all their treasure?'

'Not quite, Samantha. I think we shall leave out the threatening bit for a start. Where do you get your ideas from? I thought I'd send out a few children to go and raid the other classes, saying that they're pirates and demanding treasure. I'm sure the other teachers will join in the fun. After all, it is part of Book Week.'

'Then what do we do?' asked Tom.

'We bury it in a secret location; at least some of us bury it. I'm going to split the class into two teams. One team is going to bury the treasure, and then make a treasure map of the school to show where their treasure is buried. Then the other team will see if they can find it.'

Class Five gazed at Miss Pandemonium as if they were looking at an angel who worked miracles. 'That's brilliant,' breathed Neil. 'It will be fantastic.'

'What about The Earwig?' asked Tina. 'The Earwig won't like it at all.'

'The Earwig?' repeated Miss Pandemonium, with a tiny smile.

'Oh, sorry, miss.' Tina

turned bright red. 'I meant Mrs Earwigger.'

'I would never have guessed. Don't worry about Mrs Earwigger. I'm sure she'll think it's all great fun. Now, come with me and help get the stuff from the ambulance.'

Most of the children spent the rest of the morning hammering and sticking and cutting and measuring and painting. But the most fun was had by the raiders. For some reason Miss Pandemonium decided that Samantha Boggis wouldn't be a very good raider, or perhaps it was that she thought Samantha Boggis would be *too* good. Instead she chose three children who normally didn't get much of a look-in.

Ryan, Clyde and Linda were the terrifying trio. They decided they would start with easy pickings and they headed

straight for Mrs Patel's class of four- and five-year-olds. Outside Mrs Patel's classroom door the pirate raiders had a long argument about whether or not they should knock.

'It's stupid,' grumbled Clyde. 'Real pirates would never knock first.'

'But we're not actually real pirates, not really real, and you know what Mrs Earwigger does if you don't knock first.' Linda was nervously chewing her nails.

'Suppose we knock and then rush in quickly?' suggested Ryan.

But before they were able to do anything, the door opened and Mrs Patel stood there, smiling down at them. 'Hello, you three. Did you want something? You've been standing outside arguing for ages. We wondered what was going on, didn't we, children?'

Twenty-seven tiny faces turned and gazed at the three pirates standing by the door. Linda chewed her nails even more nervously. Ryan coughed and went red. Clyde summoned up all his courage.

'Please, miss, we're pirates,' he whispered, staring hard at the floor.

'What was that?' asked Mrs Patel, barely able to stop herself laughing out loud. Clyde clenched his fists.

'We're pirates!' he suddenly shouted,

with an immensely fierce scowl. 'And we've come to steal your treasure!'

'Yeah!' Ryan waved his pirate sword menacingly. Linda now had no nails left at all.

'Oh dear, children! I think we're being robbed by pirates!' Mrs Patel raised both arms in the air in surrender. 'You'd better come in,' she said, and led the way into the classroom. Mrs Patel went across to her desk and picked up an old biscuit tin, in which she kept emergency plasters and extra shoelaces and other useful things. 'This is my treasure tin,' she said. 'You can take this, but only if you leave us in peace.'

Clyde seized the tin. 'Thanks, Mrs Patel, that's great – I mean, yeah, and nobody move or the dame gets it!' He wasn't quite sure if pirates spoke like this or not, but at least it made him sound mean and

dangerous. The pirates backed out of the room, pulled the door shut and raced off. They didn't stop till they were safely out of sight of Mrs Patel's classroom.

'Brilliant!' cried Ryan. 'We did it! We've got some treasure.'

'Can we go now?' whispered Linda.

'No way. We've got to get some more.' Clyde was already busy scheming. Flushed with the success of their first raid he grew bolder. 'Let's rob Mr Kuddle!'

Ryan's jaw dropped and Linda suddenly needed to go to the toilet, desperately. The boys stood and waited. Linda hoped that the raid would be over by the time she returned and was disappointed to find the boys still politely waiting for her.

The three pirates crept up to Mr Kuddle's office. This time even Clyde was sure that they ought to knock first, so he

rapped loudly on the door and they burst in.

Mr Kuddle was half way through eating a cheese and tomato sandwich. He couldn't say much, at least not without quite a lot of cheese falling out of his mouth. 'Ah!' he managed.

'We're pirates!' cried Clyde. 'Give us all your treasure!'

'Please,' began Mr Kuddle, swallowing hard. 'Let's be friends. Call me Kevin . . .'

'Please, Kevin,' repeated Clyde. 'Give us all your treasure.'

'Right, ah, well, let's see.' Mr Kuddle began fishing in his pockets for loose change. He didn't seem to have quite the right idea. 'Are you collecting for charity? Which one is it?'

'We're pirates,' repeated Clyde, and he and Ryan waved their swords, while Linda

anxiously peered at Mr Kuddle over
Ryan's shoulder.

'Of course – you're from Miss
Pandemonium's class, aren't you?' smiled
Mr Kuddle.

'We're from Captain Blackbeard's pirate
galleon!' corrected Clyde. 'And if you don't

hand over some treasure quick, I'll slice your ears off!'

'Ooooh!' squeaked Linda, and hurried back to the toilet.

Mr Kuddle looked suitably horrified and, after a quick glance round his room, handed over the little silver trophy that the football team had won that spring. 'Please don't slice my ears off,' he pleaded.

'We won't,' snarled Ryan. 'Not this time . . . Kevin.'

The Class Five raiders made one more swoop, this time on Miss Goodly, who immediately offered to hand over her entire class to the pirates because, she said, her children were all 'little treasures'.

Clyde didn't have an answer to this, but Ryan threatened to tie her up and make her walk the gangplank unless she gave them some proper treasure. Miss Goodly

quickly gave them a box of giant pearls disguised as marbles, and the two boys returned to their classroom triumphant.

'Where's Linda?' asked Miss Pandemonium. 'I hope she hasn't been captured.'

'No, she went to the toilet, miss,' explained Clyde, and the class set about sorting through the treasure, ready for burying.

# 5 Tricky Tracey

Miss Pandemonium thought it would be a good idea if the treasure was hidden straight after lunch. Samantha Boggis led the burying party and, having threatened the other team with instant death if they tried to spy on her, she set off with her pirates to bury their treasure.

'Where are we going?' asked Mike.

'Somewhere the others will never think of looking, never dare to look.'

'Such as?'

'Shut up, I'll have to think.' They peered into the hall, but Mrs Earwigger was in there taking a PE lesson with Class Six. The children watched in fascination as eleven totally silent children climbed up ropes, balanced on benches and did

forward rolls on the mats.

'How does she get them so quiet?' whispered Cleo. 'It's not natural.'

'And what's happened to the rest of the class?' asked Mike.

Samantha simply pointed to the far end of the hall. A long line of twenty-one children stood silently facing the wall, with their hands on their heads.

At that moment, Mrs Earwigger gave a

shrill cry and another child joined the wall-watchers. 'By the time The Earwig has taken PE for ten minutes the whole class will be standing there,' muttered Samantha. 'Come on, there's no time to lose. I've just had a brilliant idea.'

'What? What is it?' The treasure buriers hurried after their leader, all wanting to know what she was up to. She grinned back over her shoulder at them and stopped outside Class Six.

'We're going to bury our treasure here – in The Earwig's classroom. The others may discover where it's hidden, but they'll never dare try and get it while The Earwig's in there!'

Samantha was perfectly correct in her thinking. Nobody in their right mind would go into The Earwig's class while she was there.

'Cleo, Mike – you keep a look out.'

Clutching the treasure chest, Samantha and her horde hurried into Class Six and gazed round for a suitable hiding place. There were neat piles of clothes on the desks, which the children had changed out of for PE.

'They've folded their clothes!' Tom couldn't believe his eyes. 'Every single thing – even their socks! That is weird, and I mean weird!'

'Everyone goes weird in here,' said Ravi, making it sound as if you might well catch the plague or yellow fever.

Samantha's gaze fell upon the big cupboard in the corner. Inside were tins of paint, paper, pencils, rulers, books, scissors – all sorts. She stretched up as high as she

could manage and, with
an enormously
satisfied grin, pushed
the chest on to the
top shelf. There
was a scuffle at
the door.

'Earwig's
coming!' hissed
Mike. 'Scram!'

The children
just had time to shut the cupboard door
and slip out of the room before Mrs
Earwigger appeared, followed by a neat
line of girls and a neat line of boys – all
silent. From their hiding place in the
cloakroom, Samantha and her gang
watched Class Six file into their classroom.
The door closed.

'Brilliant!' she chuckled. 'I can't wait!

Let's get back to the classroom and draw the map.'

The treasure seekers were under the command of Darren and Tracey, and they set off at great speed and with high hopes. Tom Nunnery had drawn the treasure map, and he had tried to make it look as authentic as possible. Mrs Patel's classroom had 'Here be tiny people' written across it, while Mr Kuddle's office was called 'Cave of the Big Chief'. Above Class Six it said 'Beware of the Dragon', and there was a big black cross showing that the treasure was buried in the corner of the cave.

The treasure seekers were not terribly good at map-reading, and it took them quite a while to get their bearings and work out what Tom's strange clues meant. They walked round the hall four times.

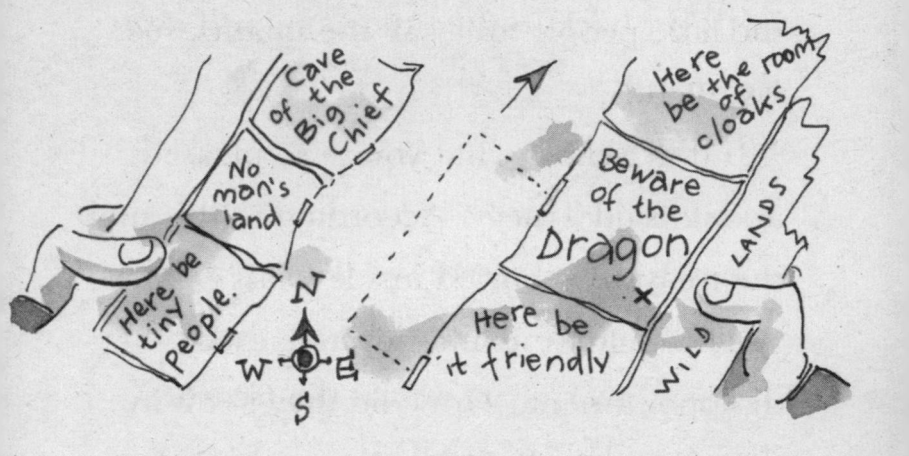

'Trouble is,' muttered Tracey, 'you can't tell which way round this map goes. Who are the little people, anyway? I reckon Samantha's just playing tricks on us.'

It was Gary who solved the problem. 'It says there's a dragon, and there's only one dragon in this school that I know of, and that's The Earwig.' They hurried down the corridor until they neared Class Six. Darren studied the map carefully.

'Yeah, look, if Class Six is where the dragon is, then Mrs Patel's would be where

the little people are – all the infants, see? Excellent!'

'I don't know what you're so pleased about,' said Tracey. 'According to this map the treasure is buried inside Class Six.'

The children could not hide their disappointment. 'How did they get it in there?' demanded Ryan, but nobody knew. 'Well, if someone got it in there then someone must be able to get it out again,' said Ryan. 'We need a plan.' The children began thinking hard.

'We need to know exactly where the treasure is buried,' declared Tracey. 'Look, it's in this corner, on the map. What's in the corner of the classroom? Tony, you take a look.'

'Me? How?'

'Just take a quick peek through the window in the door, stupid.'

'Supposing I'm spotted?'

'You'll be OK, go on.' Darren gave
Tony a shove and Tony suddenly found
himself crouching outside Mrs Earwigger's
door.

Very, very slowly he inched
his way upwards, until his
eyes were just peeping
over the bottom
frame of the
window. He peered
into Class Six,
and met the icy
glare of the deputy head on full
red alert.

'That boy there!' The Earwig's voice
could be heard even in the cloakroom
where the other treasure seekers were now
crouching, holding their breath. The door
crashed open and Mrs Earwigger fixed

Tony with her freezing eyes. 'What do you think you are doing, Tony Williams?'

Poor Tony squeezed his eyes up tight and tried ever so hard to think of a good answer, but none came. 'I don't know, Mrs Earwigger,' he whispered.

'You don't know? I see. Did Miss Pandemonium send you?'

'Um, yes, no, yes, I mean – no.'

The deputy head grabbed Tony's shoulder in a grip of iron. 'You can stand up against the wall in my classroom until you think of a sensible answer. Go on!' Tony vanished inside and the door slammed.

'That worked really well, Tracey,' said Darren.

'Excuse me,' said Tracey. 'Do you have any better ideas? Anyhow, I saw a big cupboard in the corner when Mrs

Earwigger opened the door. I bet they've hidden the treasure chest in the cupboard. How can we get the Earwig out of the classroom, so that we can get inside?'

'Give her a message,' said Gary. 'Tell her Mr Kuddle needs to see her, or something.' The treasure seekers looked at Gary. This was about the third good idea he'd had in two days. Obviously he was a lot cleverer than they gave him credit for.

'Excellent idea,' said Tracey. 'OK, a message – how about "Mr Kuddle says there is an important telephone message for you"? Then she'll have to go all the way down to the office and back again. That's plenty of time. Let's go!'

The others stared at

her. 'Your idea,' they said. 'You do it.'

Tracey mumbled a few dark threats but she knew she didn't have much choice. She took a deep breath and approached the dragon's lair.

Outside the door she stopped and glanced back at the cloakroom. 'Go on!' hissed Darren and Gary. Tracey swallowed hard and knocked. She heard footsteps clicking towards the door. The handle rattled. The door opened, and Tracey's heart stopped.

'Yes? What is it now?'

'Please, Mrs Earwigger, Mr Kuddle says that there is an important telephone message for you.'

'Really? Why did he send you? Why didn't he come himself?'

'I – I don't know,' stammered Tracey, 'I was with the secretary and the phone rang

and then he came in and saw me and sent me up here to you.' Tracey was astonished at her own boldness. The deputy head glanced back at her class.

'Not a word while I'm out of the room,' she ordered. 'Get on with your maths.'

Mrs Earwigger strode off down the corridor. The moment the deputy had disappeared round the corner the treasure seekers dashed out from the cloakroom and raced into her classroom. As they poured in through the door they suddenly realized that they had not taken into account one small problem. They had got rid of Mrs Earwigger, but they hadn't got rid of Mrs Earwigger's class. Year Six glared at them menacingly. 'What do you lot want?' demanded John. Once again Tracey's brain started working overtime.

'Us? Miss Pandemonium sent us to fetch

something. She said it was in this cupboard.' Tracey smiled and stepped towards the cupboard. John slowly got to his feet, and so did several other class members.

'Oh really? What was it?'

'Paint,' said Tracey, pulling open a door and spotting several tins of the stuff on the shelves. 'She said she'd run out of Leaf Green.' Tracey's quick eye also saw the treasure chest on the top shelf, and she winked at the others. Class Six were very

suspicious. They didn't seem to believe Tracey at all. 'Oh look!' she suddenly cried, pointing out through the classroom window, and as Class Six turned away she put a foot on the bottom shelf and heaved herself up towards the treasure.

'What?' growled John, gazing out of the window.

'A bird, I saw a bird – big – a huge bird, an ostrich probably . . .' Tracey's voice was rather muffled by the cupboard and John turned back to see what was going on.

'Oi! Get down! You can't do that!' cried John, and he threw himself towards the cupboard and tried to wrench Tracey away. Half of Class Six plunged after him, while the small gang of treasure seekers desperately tried to make their escape.

Tracey clung to the top shelf, but as John pulled harder and harder at her legs

the whole cupboard
began to topple
forward. Paper,
pencils and tins
of paint slid
from the
shelves and
cascaded
down on to
the floor.
Suddenly,

Tracey let go with a
yell and the cupboard rocked back into
place. But the damage was done. Paint tins
crashed to the floor and their lids pinged
off, scattering powder colours everywhere.
Sheets of paper were strewn far and wide.
Tracey and the gang fought to escape, but
the more they fought the more Class Six
piled on top of them and the more things

flew about the room. A rainbow-coloured cloud of paint powder swirled up into the air.

And then a huge, black vulture swept into the room. Mrs Earwigger had returned.

# 6 Mrs Earwigger's Revenge

Even above the shrieks and screams of the
multicoloured children, Mrs Earwigger's
whistle could be heard. The squirming pile
stopped wriggling and a deathly silence fell
across the classroom. Terrified faces
peered up at her. The deputy head stood
in the doorway with her eyes on stalks and
her beehive hairdo quivering with a
mixture of rage and horror.

'What is going on?' she hissed and
immediately held up both hands. 'No – I
don't want to hear a word of excuse,
nothing. This behaviour is intolerable.
Tracey Perkins, Darren Wellbrook – I take
it that is you underneath all that paint
powder – you're not even in my class.

What's been going on? No – don't tell me – out to the hall, all of you – and my class too. Go on, hands on heads, walking – go and stand in the hall while I fetch Mr Kuddle and Miss Pandemonium. We'll soon get to the bottom of this and then there'll be trouble. If you think any of you have seen me at my worst then you are in for a very nasty shock! Go on – move!'

Thirty paint-spattered children trailed into the hall and lined up along the wall. The double doors banged

and back came Mrs Earwigger, her face like a hurricane, dragging a bemused Mr Kuddle and Miss Pandemonium in her wake.

The inquisition began, and Mrs Earwigger soon discovered the cause of the chaos.

'This is absolutely appalling,' declared the deputy. 'Are you telling me that some children from Class Five hid treasure in my cupboard, and that these silly children here tried to sneak in and get it back?' Tracey, Darren and the rest of the treasure seekers shuffled their feet and nodded glumly. 'Mr Kuddle, can you believe such a thing?'

The head teacher didn't appear quite so horrified as his deputy. 'Well, actually, it sounds rather fun to me.'

'Fun? FUN?!?'

'Yes. I think it was rather a clever place to hide the treasure. After all, nobody would dare go into your classroom normally . . . if you see what I mean . . .' Mr Kuddle swallowed hard as he felt Mrs Earwigger's eyes upon him.

'It was a harmless bit of fun for Book Week,' explained Miss Pandemonium. 'It got out of hand, that's all. If the children from your class hadn't tried to stop the treasure seekers everything would be all right.'

Mrs Earwigger turned her flame-thrower eyes upon Miss Pandemonium. It was a wonder her glasses didn't melt from the heat. 'Did you know about this?'

'But of course, it was my idea.' Violet looked straight back at Mrs Earwigger with her flame-proof grey eyes. 'We made a treasure chest, hid it and then drew a

map to show where it was. The treasure seekers had to find it and bring it back.'

'Fascinating,' murmured Mr Kuddle.

'Is that what schools do now?' cried Mrs Earwigger bitterly. 'Is that meant to be education?'

Miss Pandemonium remained calm. 'It involved grids, use of map keys, interpretation, logic, language, communication skills, team-work and personal initiative.' Put like this, it sounded as if the children had just completed the Duke of Edinburgh Award Scheme. 'It was clever of Tracey to think of a way to get you to leave your classroom.' Miss Pandemonium gave the deputy a broad smile. 'You must admit, Mrs Earwigger, that it has been rather fun.'

'Fun?!?' exploded the deputy yet again. 'My classroom is a rubbish tip!'

'The treasure seekers can help clear up your room, Mrs Earwigger. Now, if you'll excuse me I must get back to the rest of my pirates.'

Miss Pandemonium trotted off across the hall and disappeared back to her classroom. Outside her door Tony Williams was waiting for her. He had an enormous grin right across his face and was clutching a big box. 'Look, miss – I got the treasure chest!'

'Tony! Well done. How on earth did you manage that?'

'Well, when Mrs Earwigger started fuming and frothing she sent all the children out to the hall, but she forgot all about me because I was still standing in the corner at the back. So I just went to the cupboard and got the treasure chest.'

'Brilliant! What a wonderful day we've had. It's almost home-time, so clear everything away. Don't forget it's Dressing-up Day tomorrow. I want to see thirty wonderful pirates. If today was a good day, then tomorrow is going to be fantabu-wonderlasticallytremendiddlyendous!'

The following morning, Witts End Primary School looked totally different. A crowd of excited children sat in the hall, waiting for assembly, wearing costumes of

all kinds, sizes and colours. Michelle had even brought her uncle's monkey at last, although it wasn't a real one. It was a rather tattered cloth monkey, with one ear missing. Michelle's uncle still went to sleep with it at night.

The only person not in fancy dress was Mrs Earwigger, but instead of wearing a costume the deputy head was wearing something far more unexpected and astonishing – a smile.

'Nice to see her looking cheerful for once,' the secretary said to Snow White, alias Mrs Patel.

'Yes, I wonder what she's been up to.'

Mr Kuddle entered the hall and assembly began. He was dressed up himself, as Widow Twankey, although his bushy moustache was a bit of a give-away. He told the children about the timetable

for the day. 'As you know, it is our Library
Opening Day today, and the Mayor has
kindly agreed to come along and perform
the opening ceremony. I am sure he will be
delighted to see such a wonderful display
of fancy dress. Don't forget that there will
be prizes for the best costumes. The
newspapers are coming too and they will

be taking photographs. It is going to be a
very exciting morning, so remember to
behave well in front of our distinguished
visitors and . . .'

At that moment the double doors at the
rear of the hall burst open and Mrs
Earwigger hurried in. She was waving
both her arms frantically at Widow
Twankey, and Mr Kuddle's voice trailed
away. The deputy head hurried up
the length of the hall

and then began a long, whispered conversation with Mr Kuddle. He frowned, groaned and raised his eyes heavenwards in complete dismay. Then he turned and faced the children.

'I'm very sorry,' he began. 'There has been a bit of a mix-up. Mrs Earwigger says the secretary has just received a telephone call from the Town Hall to say that the Mayor cannot come today because of more important commitments. He's sorry, but he won't be able to open the new library after all.'

The disappointment among the children was huge. A groan went up that would have made the hardest heart weep. Poor Mr Kuddle struggled to think of something that might help to save the situation. He raised a hand for some quiet.

'Don't forget that we still have our lovely

costumes, and the press will still be coming to take photograaa . . .'

Mrs Earwigger whispered into the head's ear once again, and he turned away in despair. This time it was the deputy who spoke to the hall. 'Since the Mayor is unable to come there really is no point in the press coming to take pictures, so I telephoned the newspaper offices and cancelled their visit. I am very much afraid, children, that nobody is coming here today at all.'

Violet Pandemonium was watching Mrs Earwigger very carefully, and wondering why the deputy head seemed somehow pleased. Although Mrs Earwigger was looking at the children very seriously, there was something about her that made Violet think she was just acting. Very quietly, she slipped from her chair and hurried down

the empty corridor to the secretary's office.

'Isn't it awful,' said the secretary. 'The children must be so disappointed. I couldn't believe it when Mrs Earwigger came in and told me that the Mayor had cancelled and she had to cancel the newspapers.'

Miss Pandemonium took a deep breath. Everything was beginning to make sense. 'I thought the Mayor had rung you?' she said to the secretary.

'Oh no.'

'Quick, ring the Town Hall! There's something fishy going on.'

The secretary hastily dialled the Town Hall and Miss Pandemonium seized the phone and began firing questions at the poor official at the other end. After several minutes, Violet slammed the phone back down. 'Mrs Earwigger has made the whole thing up. She rang the Town Hall late yesterday and said that we had to cancel. Now the Mayor has gone off shopping for some new trousers. Mrs Earwigger has made the whole thing up!'

'How could she? I mean, why? What shall we do? The poor children . . .' moaned the secretary, but Miss Pandemonium was not going to be defeated.

'You telephone the press and get them back here on the double. I shall sort out the Mayor!'

Miss Pandemonium raced back up the

corridor and burst into the hall, which was still a scene of doom and gloom. 'Excuse me, Mr Kuddle,' cried Violet. 'Small emergency – must dash – I shall be back very shortly – keep the children in the hall – Samantha, Gary, Mike, Laura, Ravi, Kimberley, you come with me, quick, on the double, come on, and bring your swords!' And with that Miss Pandemonium and her pirate gang hurried out to her ambulance. A few moments later, with siren blaring and lights flashing, the ambulance was screaming towards the centre of town.

# 7 The Pirates Go Kidnapping

'Where are we going, miss?' asked Ravi, as the ambulance tore up the High Street.

'Just keep your eyes open for the Mayor,' Miss Pandemonium answered grimly.

'There's his car!' Laura shouted suddenly. 'Look, with the little flag on the front.'

Miss Pandemonium brought the ambulance to a screeching halt behind the Mayor's big black limousine. 'Come on, he must be in the shop. We've got to get him back to school as quickly as possible. Raiding party – are you ready?'

'Ready, miss!'

'OK – follow me!'

Waving their wooden swords ferociously,

the pirate gang piled out of the ambulance and burst into the department store, much to the surprise and horror of the customers. 'He'll be in the Menswear bit!' cried Violet, and promptly went dashing up the down escalator the wrong way. The smaller pirates followed on the proper escalator and were at the top long before Violet arrived, puffing and panting.

Safe in his office, the store manager was on the telephone to the police. 'Yes,' he hissed. 'It's a raid! They're disguised as pirates. Quick – for heaven's sake get up here at once!'

Up in the Menswear Department the Mayor had found a rather nice pair of trousers and had wandered off to the changing room to try them on.

'There he goes!' pointed Kimberley. 'Over there, miss!'

'Come on!' yelled Samantha and without further ado she dashed across to the changing rooms. As the seven pirates launched their ambush, panic broke out. Several men came running out of the changing rooms clutching half-undone trousers and shirts. The poor Mayor had only just taken off his old pair of trousers when he was set upon by the pirates, whisked off his feet, and carried away, shouting for help and waving his hairy legs in mid-air.

'I want my trousers back! This is outrageous! I am the Mayor – put me down!'

'Quieten down, you scum!' roared Samantha in her fiercest pirate voice, 'or I'll cut off your ears!'

'Ooooh,' squeaked the Mayor, and he went deathly quiet at once.

Several staff and customers tried to come to the Mayor's rescue, rushing upon the kidnappers and attacking them with an array of coat hangers, hat stands, umbrellas and handbags. The pirates, though, had had far more practice in the school playground and easily kept their attackers at bay.

Once outside, they bundled the Mayor into the ambulance. Miss Pandemonium

took off at once, with a squeal of burning rubber and clouds of smoke, closely followed by two wailing police cars, which had just arrived on the scene.

'This is brilliant!' said Gary, leaning out of the window. 'I like being a pirate.'

By the time the ambulance reached the school, the Mayor had managed to get his trousers back on and Miss Pandemonium had explained just what had been going on, and how Mrs Earwigger had tried to trick them all. 'I'm sorry,' she said, 'but there was no time to lose. I knew we just had to get you here as quickly as possible. Everyone is still at school, all dressed up and waiting for you to open the library.'

The Mayor sat next to her in the front, gripping the edge of his seat for safety as Violet flung the ambulance round a corner on two wheels. He gave her a pale, but

excited smile. 'It's great fun,' he chuckled. 'I haven't enjoyed myself so much for ages. Fancy being kidnapped by ten-year-old pirates! I wish all library-openings were like this! It's going to make a wonderful newspaper story. Quick, turn left down this alley, it's a short cut.'

Screeching into the car park, the ambulance had hardly come to a halt before everyone leapt out and went charging into school. Miss Pandemonium led the way. 'Leave the talking to me,' she hissed as they marched into the hall. A sea of expectant little faces watched.

'What's going on!' cried Mrs Earwigger. Violet gave her a little smile.

'It's quite all right, Mrs Earwigger. There has been a little bit of a mix-up. Allow me to introduce the Mayor. He has come to open the library after all.'

'But that's impossible!' spluttered the deputy. 'I shan't allow it.' Then, as if to add strength to Mrs Earwigger's words, the double doors burst open and four policemen charged into the hall.

'Hold it right there!' yelled Inspector Hole.

Mr Kuddle, or rather Widow Twankey, stepped forward with a remarkably cheerful smile. 'What – more fancy dress?' he began. 'Isn't that nice, children? The newspaper reporters have dressed up too.'

'I'm not a reporter, I'm a real policeman!' screamed Inspector Hole, 'and

you are under arrest for kidnapping, assault, speeding and and and . . .'

Inspector Hole suddenly stopped and eyed Mr Kuddle with undisguised horror.

'You're the headmaster! You've got a moustache!'

'That's right.'

'You're wearing a dress!'

'Yes. Can I have a go on your whistle?'

'No, stop it, put my whistle down. Arrest those pirates!'

The policemen waded in among the children and were about to arrest the pirates when the Mayor came to the rescue. He hastily explained to the inspector that he was at the school to open the library, that it was Dressing-up Day, and so on. Calm began to descend. Only Mrs Earwigger was becoming more and more worked up as she realized her plan was about to fail.

Just as the deputy was going into her mouth-disappearing act and getting ready to have a minor explosion, a rescue party arrived in the shape of the real reporter and photographer. As soon as the deputy head saw the press cameras, her whole attitude changed and her face beamed a bright smile. She simpered ever so sweetly,

patted her hair into place and hurried across the hall. 'Ah, dear gentlemen of the press – you've come to photograph Class Six of course!'

'Well, actually, we haven't decided what . . .'

'Of course you want my class,' insisted Mrs Earwigger. 'And me too. We are by far the best dressed. Besides, we are the eldest. Come on, my class, on your feet.'

As Class Six got to their feet the other teachers and children looked desperately at each other. One moment Mrs Earwigger was trying to ruin the show and the next she was hogging the limelight. All eyes turned to Miss Pandemonium. Surely Miss Pandemonium could stop this outrage? But it wasn't Violet who came to the rescue at all, it was Widow Twankey.

'I think the Music Room would be the

best place for a photograph, Mrs Earwigger,' said Mr Kuddle. 'It's nice and quiet in there and the press can take as much time as they want. Follow me, Class Six.' The head teacher led the children out of the room. When they reached the Music Room door Mr Kuddle turned to Mrs Earwigger. 'You'd better go in and check that it's clear,' he suggested.

'I must say this is a very good idea of yours, Mr Kuddle,' said the deputy, marching into the Music Room. 'At least my class won't be disturbed by those horrible pirates.'

No sooner was she inside than Mr Kuddle pulled the door shut and locked it. 'Now,' he said calmly, 'let's all go back to the hall and do what we want to do for a change.' He led the children back to the

hall, ignoring the muffled cries from inside the sound-proofed Music Room.

After that, the library opening ceremony went very well indeed. The Mayor made a funny speech, invited all the policemen in, and everyone ate cake. The press took so many photographs the school ended up with a double-page spread in the newspaper.

It was all rather enjoyable, but what everyone noticed most of all was how relaxing it was, how jolly everyone felt, how helpful and thoughtful everyone was, now that Mrs Earwigger was shut in the Music Room. 'I suppose someone ought to let her out,' said Mrs Patel.

'I've lost the key,' snapped Widow Twankey. After years of putting up with Mrs Earwigger, Mr Kuddle wasn't going to let her off that easily.

'I'll save her a piece of cake,' said Miss Pandemonium quietly.

As it happened, Mrs Earwigger would have found it difficult to come out even if she had wanted to. Stuck inside the Music Room, she had become desperate to escape, but apart from the locked door the only way out was through a window in the flat roof which was too high for her to reach.

Looking around, Mrs Earwigger noticed a pile of drums. There were four altogether, starting with a little snare drum and going up to the big bass drum. The deputy reckoned that if she put one drum on top of the other she could climb up, stand on the top and reach the window — and freedom.

Making the drum-mountain was easy. Climbing up the mountain with her dress

hitched up round her knees was a bit more difficult. Balancing on the top of the wobbly mountain while trying to open a window was very difficult indeed. The pile began to quiver and quake, with Mrs Earwigger frantically dancing about on the

summit, trying to stay upright —
unsuccessfully.

'Aaaaaaargh!'

With a thunderous crash Mrs
Earwigger's feet disappeared through the
top drum. Then her whole body came
crashing after her feet, pushing her down
inside all four drums, pinning her arms to
her sides and leaving her barely able to
move.

And that was how they found her at
half-past three after the children had gone
home. Mr Kuddle, who by this time had
changed back into his normal clothes,
found the key and unlocked the Music
Room door. He peered inside. 'Well, it
looks as if Mrs Earwigger has decided to
come in fancy dress after all.'

From between the top two drums a tiny
chink allowed Mrs Earwigger to peer out

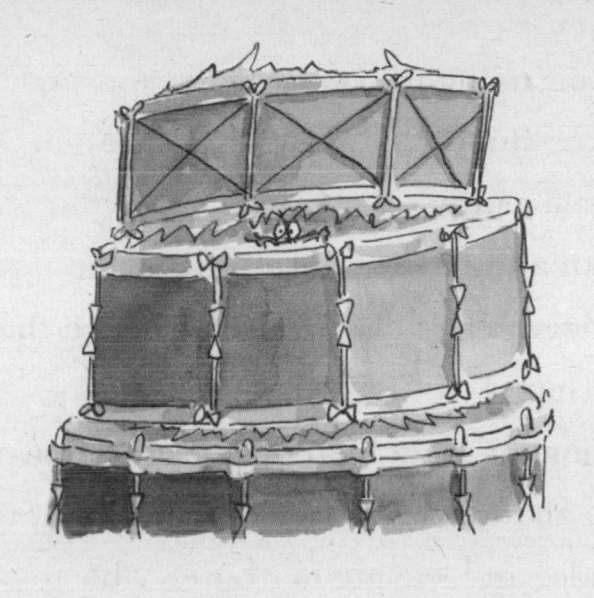

helplessly. 'Out of my way!' she hissed
furiously.

'Would you like some help to get out of
those drums?' Miss Goodly asked.

'Just get out of my way!' cried the
deputy once again and the mountain of
drums began to slowly shuffle across the
floor towards them. In astonished silence
the staff stood back and watched as the
drum-pile set off along the corridor and
headed home.

Mr Kuddle watched her go and smiled cheerfully. Somehow he reckoned that when Mrs Earwigger returned to the school – if she returned – she would not be nearly so troublesome. And if she was, well, he could always call on Violet Pandemonium to come and sort things out.

# 14½ Things You Didn't Know About

# Jeremy Strong

* * * * * * * * * * * * * * * * * *

1. He loves eating liquorice.

2. He used to like diving. He once dived from the high board and his trunks came off!

3. He used to play electric violin in a rock band called **THE INEDIBLE CHEESE SANDWICH**.

4. He got a 100-metre swimming certificate when he couldn't even swim.

5. When he was five, he sat on a heater and burnt his bottom.

6. Jeremy used to look after a dog that kept eating his underpants. (No – **NOT** while he was wearing them!)

7. When he was five, he left a basin tap running with the plug in and flooded the bathroom.

8. He can make his ears waggle.

9. He has visited over a thousand schools.

10. He once scored minus ten in an exam! That's ten less than nothing!

11. His hair has gone grey, but his mind hasn't.

12. He'd like to have a pet tiger.

13. He'd like to learn the piano.

14. He has dreadful handwriting.

**And a half . . .** His favourite hobby is sleeping. He's very good at it.

Pssssssssssst!

# If you love Puffin Books you should choose

### Here's what's in it for you:

⭐ 6 magazines

⭐ 6 free books a year (of your choice)

⭐ The chance to see YOUR writing in print

## PLUS

⭐ Exclusive author features

⭐ Articles

⭐ Quizzes

⭐ Competitions and games

### And that's not all.

### You get PRESENTS too.

Simply subscribe here to become a member

**puffinpost.co.uk**

and wait for your copy to decorate your doorstep.

(WARNING – reading *Puffin Post* may make you late for school.)